GREEK

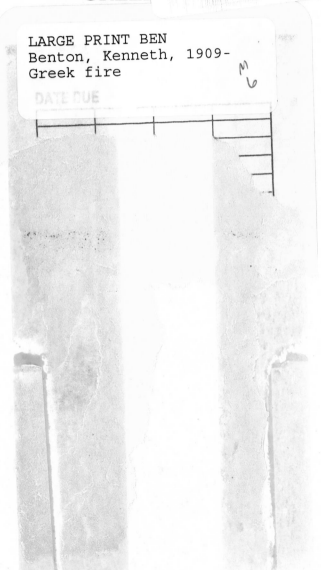

# GREEK FIRE

## Kenneth Benton

Chivers Press • G.K. Hall & Co.
Bath, England   Thorndike, Maine USA

This Large Print edition is published by Chivers Press, England, and by G.K. Hall & Co., USA.

Published in 2000 in the U.K. by arrangement with the author, c/o Juliet Burton.

Published in 2000 in the U.S. by arrangement with Juliet Burton Literary Agency.

U.K. Hardcover ISBN 0-7540-4009-7    (Chivers Large Print)
U.S. Softcover    ISBN 0-7838-8864-3    (Nightingale Series Edition)

The text of this Large Print edition is unabridged.
Other aspects of the book may vary from the original edition.

Set in 16 pt. New Times Roman.

Printed in Great Britain on acid-free paper.

**British Library Cataloguing in Publication Data available**

**Library of Congress Cataloging-in-Publication Data**

Benton, Kenneth, 1909–
    Greek fire / Kenneth Benton.
    Originally published in 1985 under the author's alternate name : James Kirton.
        p.    cm.
    ISBN 0-7838-8864-3 (lg. print : sc : alk. paper)
    1. Intelligence officers—Great Britain—Fiction.
    2. Albania—Politics and government—Fiction.
    3. Large type books.    I. Title.
    PR6052.E545 G74    2000
    823'.914—dc21                                    99–052470

# CHAPTER ONE

On the plush-carpeted tenth floor of the SIS building in Southwark, the floor where the chief, his secretariat and his special aides have their offices, there is a door marked Chief Inspector.

The chief inspector, in the Intelligence Service, is not a police officer. His task is to keep an eye on all intelligence operations abroad and the administrative sections at Head Office, and make sure that security rules are observed, complaints investigated and that officers and staff are as efficient as possible. Any adverse report on an SIS executive, any unexplained leak to the media, any intercepted foreign intelligence mentioning SIS activities, lands up on the chief inspector's desk, and his officers go into action, fast. C.I.'s deputy, at the time of these events, was Lucas Grant, and it was he who on a misty October morning was called into C.I.'s office.

Bratby looked up, frowning, and without a word passed across the desk a copy of an en clair telegram sent to the Foreign and Commonwealth Office. 'It's bad news, Luke. I'll explain when you've read it.' He rose, and went to look out of the window, through the faint mist, at the Shell Building and the distant glimpse of St Paul's.

'HEAD OF PERSONNEL, FCO. REGRET TO REPORT ROGER INGRAM HAS BEEN FOUND DROWNED OFF WEST COAST OF CORFU. INGRAM HAD BEEN MISSING SINCE SATURDAY EIGHTH OCTOBER WHEN HE WENT BATHING NEAR GLYFADA WHERE HE AND HIS WIFE WERE ON LEAVE. BODY FOUND YESTERDAY AND IDENTIFIED BY WIFE. NO SIGN OF FOUL PLAY. VICE CONSUL CORFU TAKING ALL NECESSARY ACTION. MACARTNEY, ATHENS.'

Grant was puzzled. His chief had turned round and was still frowning. 'What's wrong, Nigel? Ingram was one of ours, of course—I remember briefing him before he went to Athens, about four years ago. But surely he's been transferred to Head Office since then, hasn't he? And incidentally, I didn't know he was married.'

'He wasn't. He only met his wife after his transfer to London. I think you'd better hear the whole story from his controller.' He pressed a switch and spoke at his desk telephone. 'Lucy, ask controller/Greece to come in now, please.'

The man who came in, Robert Sankey, was middle-aged, with a pleasant, open face which at the moment was wearing a very worried expression. 'Morning, Nigel. Morning, Luke,' he said nervously, then blurted out. 'I should

2

never have let him go. I'm afraid I've let you in for an awful can of worms, Nigel.'

'Sit down, Robert,' said C.I. gently. 'No one's blaming you for anything so far. Just tell Luke the whole story, from the beginning. I haven't told him anything yet.'

'OK.' He turned to Grant. 'Ingram worked a three-year posting in Athens. He had a delicate job to do, and did it very well. But we couldn't risk declaring him to the Greeks. As far as they were concerned—and the Soviets, too, we hoped—he was just another First Secretary in our Embassy.'

Grant raised a hand. 'Why exactly couldn't you declare him to the Greeks? You have a liaison with their Intelligence, haven't you?'

'Because, as I said, it was a very delicate job he was doing, and although our relations with the Greeks are good we couldn't be sure someone, somewhere down the line, wouldn't leak to the Russians, and that'd have been disastrous.' Grant nodded, and Sankey went on, a little calmer now. 'This was the job. One of the KGB chaps in the legal residency in Athens—Major Nikolai Vlasov, with cover as Second Secretary, Information, in the Soviet Embassy—was working on a ploy we very much wanted to know about, and when I say 'we' I don't only mean HMG, but NATO Directorate of Intelligence. One of Vlasov's agents is a Greek journalist named Spiro Katastari, whose task is to explore links between the Greek minority in Southern Albania—there are forty thousand of them—and their relatives in Greece. Katastari is a talent-spotter only—trust the KGB not to let anyone know too much. When he finds someone with relatives in Albania, someone who can be worked on through family feelings or the prospect of hard cash, he vets him as best as he can by getting to know him and then fingers him to Vlasov, who takes it from there, using skilled local recruiters, I suppose. But that's all we know. We couldn't discover the object of the exercise. When Ingram finished his tour in Athens last year we let his assistant, who's a very bright girl and keen on action, take over his job as case-officer for Katastari.'

'*Case-officer?* You mean Katastari's a double agent, working for both Vlasov and you?'

'Yes, but we've every reason to think his main loyalty—which I may add is highly rewarded—is to us, and that Vlasov hasn't a clue about his contacts with Jenny. That's the girl—Jenny Otfield.'

Grant looked, as he felt, baffled. 'But if Otfield is running this double now, and has been for the past year, how does Ingram come into the picture?' He started. 'You can't mean you allowed Ingram to keep in touch with an agent while someone else was handling him? It'd be breaking a cardinal rule, and you know it, man.'

The chief inspector saw Sankey's face going first red, then pale and angry, and intervened. 'You're rushing your fences, Luke. Let him explain.'

'I'm sorry. Go ahead, Robert.'

'The point is Katastari's a Greek, so he doesn't take too well to the idea of being run by a woman. It wasn't Jenny's fault, from what head of Athens station told me; she was handling the man very well. But he got wind of Ingram's visit to Corfu, and wormed his holiday address out of Jenny, saying he wanted to send him his best wishes for the married state, or something like that, and Jenny— reluctantly, I'd imagine, but for the sake of her relations with him—let him have his way, only insisting that if he wrote to Roger it should be something quite innocuous and not signed with his own name. It seemed quite a reasonable request for Katastari to make. After all, he and Roger Ingram had worked together for three years, and although they could only meet in secret they were friends.' Sankey saw the disapproving look on Grant's face and hurried on. 'But it wasn't just good wishes that Spiro sent. It was a message, all wrapped up in double-speak, about having found the solution to the chess problem he and Roger had puzzled over so long, and that as he'd shortly be visiting Corfu on holiday he'd get in touch. He added that Roger would be absolutely fascinated by the solution. The letter was signed with a pseudonym known only to them both.'

Grant said mildly, 'Not very good tradecraft, was it? Short-circuiting his case-officer like that? Katastari had had field training, I suppose?'

The chief inspector said, 'Let him get on with it,' and Grant subsided.

Sankey said, 'He had been trained and it wasn't good tradecraft, but to continue: Ingram couldn't write to the man direct and tell him to hand over whatever it was to the girl, so he ought to have let Spiro know through Jenny that he didn't want any contact with him. But . . .' Sankey looked appealingly at Grant. 'You know how it is, Luke. God knows you've had enough field experience yourself. Every case-officer believes he's the only one who really understands his agent, and that anyone else will make a balls of the relationship sooner or later. And of course Ingram was mad keen to find out what the 'solution' was. So he found someone in Corfu who was flying to Athens the next day—an English friend he could rely on—and gave him a letter to deliver to the Embassy, addressed to head of station. More wrapping up, of course, but he reported what had happened and said he proposed to see the chap, take what he had to offer, and give him a raspberry for going over Jenny's head. And that,' concluded Sankey, 'is all we know. Head of station sent us an immediate signal explaining what had happened, but before we could reply the Embassy had wired the Office with the news of the death.'

Grant nodded. 'C.I. showed me the cable. Did they say they were going to send Miss Otfield to investigate the death on the spot?'

Sankey looked at him in surprise. 'It'd be too dangerous, Luke. You see, Jenny's not in Consular Department at the Embassy, she's Commercial. So why should she be making enquiries about the death of a Brit sub?'

'I see. You don't think it was an accident, do you, Robert?'

'No, I don't. Why should this happen just at the moment when Ingram was expecting to meet Katastari and receive vital information? No, I'm afraid I think Roger was murdered, but if so why? Murder is going a bit far, even for the Russians. We don't usually liquidate each other's officers. There's something very odd about this. It may be Katastari lured Ingram into a trap, and he took a gun along with him—he'd be a bloody fool not to—and they knocked him off before he could use it. The thing is, how do we find out? Personnel have offered to send out someone, which is decent of them but it wouldn't be good enough. We need someone who's an investigator—an SIS investigator, I mean—and who's clean as far as my parts of the world are concerned. I'd go myself, but I'm declared

7

to the Greeks and the moment I started asking questions they'd get very interested indeed. So would the Soviets.' He stopped and looked at Grant hopefully, rather like a dog suggesting it was time to be taken for a walk.

'I've got a trip to India lined up for next Thursday,' said Grant.

'It's only a question of a couple of days, Luke,' said Bratby, still at the window. 'And it's true you're clean, as far as this thing is concerned. You've always been connected with Western stations.' He meant Western Europe and the Americas. 'I don't suppose you even speak Greek.'

'Apart from vestigial traces of the classical idiom used by Pliny,' said Grant with a touch of sarcasm, 'I haven't a word. I don't think I'm a good choice, you know,' he added, turning to Bratby. 'The whole areas's a closed book to me.'

'But you could have an interpreter,' suggested Sankey eagerly. 'Someone in the know, of course.'

Grant looked at him sharply. 'Like Miss Otfield?' he asked. 'Is that it?' Bratby was looking out of the window again. This suggestion wasn't new to him, obviously.

'She speaks very fluent demotic Greek and is not blown to the Greeks,' explained Sankey. 'Your cover could be as a member of Personnel, FCO, arriving in time for the funeral with messages from Roger's friends in

8

the Office and of course you'd want to see that Clare Ingram is all right, as far as she can be.' Sankey saw the look on Grant's face and hurried on. 'I know I ought to have prevented this happening. He told me he'd taken this villa in Corfu for his honeymoon and I ought to have warned him that Katastari might try and contact him. But of course I thought the man was in Athens and unlikely to find out about Roger's visit. All the same I should have told him flatly it wasn't on. If I had, he mightn't be dead now.'

Grant saw the misery in the man's face and relented. 'You couldn't have known,' he said gently.

'I had no right to take the risk. It's such a bloody waste,' Sankey burst out suddenly. 'Roger was a first-class man, just the type we want for the Middle Eastern stations, and God knows it's difficult to find the right man these days. And Clare, too. I didn't get to know her well, but she seemed to be just the calm, sophisticated type of girl who'd stand all the strains and stresses without losing her cool. A beauty, too—not pretty, just beautiful. And obviously in love with Roger. Poor Clare! The bottom'll have dropped out of her world.'

At last the chief inspector turned round and came back to his desk. One glance at Grant's face was enough. Sankey's obvious distress had done more than any reasoned argument. 'Are you quite happy to go, Luke?'

9

Grant wriggled his shoulders. 'I'm not happy, for God's sake, because I loathe going to a place I know nothing about and where I can't speak the language. But of course I'll go.' He turned to Sankey. 'Give me a letter for Clare Ingram, and I'll take it with me. Can your people get me the ticket for the first flight tomorrow, and arrange with the MO for jabs tonight, if necessary. I'm OK for cholera and TAB. Do I need a visa?'

'No. And you won't need any jabs either. I'm very grateful, Luke. It shouldn't delay your Indian trip. Just find out what you can from the V-C and Clare. Jenny'll help. She's a splendid girl, gutsy and with a lot of common sense. You'd better pretend to know her quite well already. Then it'll seem natural for you to be seen together. Come down to my room and I'll give you more briefing on Soviet/Albanian relations. Anything else?'

'Yes. A good guide to Corfu.'

The chief inspector watched them go. He smiled.

\*     \*     \*

In all Russian embassies the KGB officers are only allowed to work in the dismal *referentura*, which consists of a number of sound-proofed offices, artificially lit and ventilated, to which access is obtained through an ante-room, guarded around the clock by armed operatives, and a steel, bomb-proof door. All the windows are bricked up to foil long-range photographic and electronic snoopers.

In Athens, life in the Embassy *referentura* was particularly hard, for the 'legal resident', Colonel Andreev, was a slave-driver, and his minions were bitterly envious of colleagues in the 'illegal residency'—whom of course they were not allowed to meet who worked under commercial cover as TASS or shipping representatives in Piraeus, and who had to be allowed a certain degree of freedom to mix with the locals and enjoy what Greece had to offer. Even greater envy would have been aroused by the knowledge that one member of their group, Nikolai Vlasov, lived two hundred miles away in Corfu, playing the part of a rich Italian with a handsome seaside villa.

But Vlasov's operation was known only to his chief, Andreev, and the cipher clerks in the Athens *referentura*. Andreev sat in his stuffy office for long hours like a spider in the centre of his web. He was not in a good temper when he pressed the desk buzzer and told his secretary to bring in Major Vlasov, who had been summoned to Athens for urgent consultation. The colonel did not like bright, know-all young officers, and especially one who had an uncle in the Politburo.

Vlasov came in, saluted, and remained standing. He was not invited to sit down.

Andreev looked up from the report he had

been reading. 'Why was it necessary to liquidate this man? He could have been a mine of information if properly interrogated. It seems to me you acted very harshly, Nikolai Viktorich.'

'I will explain, Comrade Colonel,' said Vlasov, and did so at length, in a text-book style that could not be faulted.

Grudgingly, Colonel Andreev nodded. 'You seem to have wriggled out of the jam neatly, Major, and I hope for your sake nothing goes wrong now. You are confident that the operation can go forward?'

'Yes, Comrade Colonel.'

'Very well. You'd better get back to Corfu. Watch your cover.' The chief seemed to have finished with him but as Vlasov, greatly relieved, turned to go the older man said quickly, *'E come stà la dolce vita di Corfu, Signor Rossi?'*

*'Come sempre, Colonello,'* drawled Vlasov, with the easy assurance of an Italian playboy. His official manner had vanished. *'C'è la vita di caffè. Si guarda le belle ragazze, si beve ouzo, e poi...'*

'That'll do, that'll do,' said his chief, a little discomfited. 'Just keep it up. This operation is only part of something much bigger, don't forget, and if we fail in our part we get blamed for the whole.'

And what on earth did that mean, thought Vlasov resentfully, as he pressed the release

12

spring of the steel door.


## CHAPTER TWO

The Trident swooped down between the steep headland of Kanoni and the gleaming hotels on the wooded promontory of Perama, skimmed along the runway beside the pale mirror of the Khalikiopoulos lagoon, and landed. In the forward cabin Luke Grant heard behind him the shattering roar of the reversed jet-streams, and felt their braking effect as the big plane slowed down and taxied sedately round to the airport building.

The sun shone and the air was soft and warm, so different from the bleak gusts of rain that Grant had left in London. The people watching the arrival from the balcony were still dressed in the casual clothes of summer and indeed many of the passengers emerging from the Trident were holiday-makers taking advantage of out-of-season package fees and the lack of congestion on the beaches.

Grant had all he needed in the holdall under his seat, and he passed quickly through the controls. At the barrier a girl was waiting. Faded blue jeans clung like a second skin to her slender legs and she was wearing an open-necked shirt and a denim jacket, with an 'ethnic' bag slung from her shoulder. She was, in fact, dressed like any other tourist of her age, as ordered by head of station in Athens.

He had said, 'I know Luke Grant quite well. As with all the Inspectorate people, his photo's in Archives, so borrow it and take it with you if you like. He's about six foot, and broad. Used to play for the Harlequins. His face has a sort of weathered look about it, perhaps because he's spent such a large part of his career in South America, and you may find he looks a bit grim. It's his solid Yorkshire background, I suppose. Nice chap, though, when you get to know him, and can be good company. He'll have a copy of your photograph to study in the plane, so he won't miss you ... Oh, another thing. Robert Sankey suggests you both act as if you were old friends, so that it'll seem another reason for you to be sent from here to interpret for him.'

Old friends, thought Jenny. What was that supposed to mean?

But head of station was smiling to himself as he remembered. 'He's a tremendous fellow in a scrap,' he added. 'I remember once in Panama ...'

Jenny let him finish his story, smiled politely and withdrew. Inwardly, she was seething. Why for God's sake pick on *her* for this job? Had the man already forgotten about her and Roger? It had only been a year since he had been posted.

She recognized Grant at once and went up

14

to him. 'Hullo, darling,' he said, dropped his bag and kissed her on both cheeks. (If they wanted him to play their silly games, so be it). Half-amused, he felt her body stiffen. Her skin was warm, sun-welcoming skin, and her hair was dark and cut to shoulder-length, framing a small sensitive face that looked as if it could change from sadness to joy as unpredictably as the shifting patterns of light on the lagoon.

'It's lovely to see you, Luke,' she said, taking his arm. 'Is that all your luggage?'

'Sure. Let's get going.' They walked out into the bright autumn sunshine. Jenny said, 'I've booked a room for you at the Cavalieri. It's old-fashioned but nice, with a lovely view. I chose the second floor because it's quieter— but not too far to walk if the lift breaks down. I've got a taxi over there.'

'And where are you staying, Jenny?'

'Same hotel, same floor.'

Practical girl, thought Grant approvingly. Then he remembered that she had been Ingram's secretary, and said, 'This must be an unhappy experience for you, I'm afraid.'

Jenny said nothing for a moment. They got into the taxi and she gave directions. Then she said levelly, 'Yes, it is. I knew him well, you see.'

'I'm sorry we have to go through with this silly farce. It wasn't my idea, and I don't think it's necessary.'

'I'll explain later. But I'm afraid we have to

15

put up with it, and just act like old friends, or relations.'

Grant laughed. 'That remark is unanswerable.'

'What d'you mean?'

'If I say, Thank God, we only have to be friends, it's insulting. If I say, What a pity, I was hoping for so much more, you'd slap my face.'

'I certainly would.' But she smiled, too, and her small face lit up.

They were approaching the outskirts of the town when Grant asked, 'When is the body to be shipped back to England?'

'It isn't. Roger's going to be buried here. It was in the local paper this morning.' She glanced at her watch. 'In half an hour, at the British Cemetery.'

Grant thought for a moment. 'I'd like to be there, just as an onlooker. Will you come, too?'

'No ... No, I'd rather go to the hotel and wait for you there. I—er—can't go to the funeral in these clothes, and there's hardly time to change, so if it's all right with you—?'

'Of course.' He wondered what her real reason was. 'But could you drop me there?'

She nodded, and told the driver to turn left when he came to Koloktroni. 'I'll take your bag to the hotel.'

'That'd be fine. Thanks.'

The car stopped beside tall iron gates in a stuccoed wall. A notice read, 'British Cemetery, Corfu. Please use the entrance to your right'.

It was a wooden door, painted a faded green, with a bronze bell hanging beside it. A cheerful teenage girl let them in. There was a tangled garden and on the left a small building which obviously housed the hereditary custodian. Two old ladies dressed in black satin knitting on a bench in the sun, looking up with mild curiosity above the clicking needles. A broad grassy walk tunnelled between tall cypresses and the arching boughs of mimosa and eucalyptus.

'The grave will be up there at the far end,' said Jenny, pointing . . . 'I'll go now.'

Marble headstones tilted among the grasses, where hens were scratching placidly. An incongruous note was struck by a visitor's book on a small iron table. Grant paused to read the appreciative comments of those who had come to the cemetery—as tourists. As he did so, he glanced back. Jenny was still standing where he had left her, looking up the grassy avenue, her face taut and expressionless. She turned and went slowly to the gate.

At any other time it would have been a delightful place to spend an hour or so. The scent of late roses mingled with the tang of

17

rosemary and cypress. An air of gentle melancholy was lent by the faded inscriptions on the memorials to the British who, in the last century, had ruled the island for fifty years. Grant paused to decipher the words carved on an impressive tomb:

*Sacred to the memory of*
*The Honourable Charles Gustavus Monckton (late) Captain in H.B.M. 38th Regiment of Connaught Rangers, who died by the hand of an assassin on the 9th August 1831 aged 26 years.*
*The feeling of grief and indignation strongly and universally expressed by the Regiment was only moderated on witnessing the prompt punishment of the murderer ... who was executed on 11th August 1831.*

After the word 'murderer' the name 'Private James Clarke' was carved in very small script, as if such a man could not be given even the dignity of capital letters.

Only two days afterwards, thought Grant. In peacetime, too. Just a drumhead court-martial and a firing squad. He smiled wryly. Some would say, those were the days.

At the far end of the long walk, where a high wall divided the cemetery from the grounds of the Model Prison, was War Graves Commission territory. Rows of small crosses and tablets, neatly maintained, marked the graves of soldiers and sailors killed during, and

18

even after, both world wars.

In the angle of the cemetery wall nearest the grey roof of the prison building was a freshly-dug grave. In the distance Grant heard the deep clang of the bell by the gate.

He kept out of the way while the little procession came slowly into view between the dark, brooding cypresses and formed up around the grave. The undertakers and two Greek officials, all dressed in black, were easily recognisable. They played their parts with dignity, following the unfamiliar Anglican service with decent respect and grave faces.

Clare Ingram was dressed in something long and dark. A black veil covered her fair hair and fell over her face. There was a suggestion of remoteness about her tall figure, almost as if she did not hear the solemn words of the funeral service read by the vice-consul, a small stout man with a weather-beaten face, trim white moustache and a bearing that proclaimed 'regular soldier, retired'.

When the coffin, brash and shiny like all coffins, had been lowered into the grave and the last words said, the small group turned away and retreated down the avenue. A man who had been waiting behind a tree came forward, lit a cigarette, and hefted his spade. Grant drew near and watched the steady swing of his shoulders. The man tidied the earth and moved away, leaving a raw scar in the ground made bleaker by the few desultory flowers already fading in the warm sunlight. So this, thought Grant, was Ingram's last posting.

He turned and walked quickly down the avenue. Outside the cemetery gates the Greek officials and the undertakers were bowing to the widow, murmuring condolences. Then they went off to their cars. The vice-consul opened the door of a white Datsun, helped Clare Ingram in and spoke to her for a few moments through the open window. As she drove away and he turned towards his own Cortina, with the tiny Union Jack flying from the bonnet, Grant came forward. 'Major Barnard?' he asked. 'I'm Lucas Grant, Consular Department.'

'Grant? Oh, yes I had a cable. You're welcome, of course, but—what is this about?'

'I was coming to Corfu anyway,' explained Grant untruthfully, 'for a few days leave, and the Office asked me to see if I could do anything to help.' He had scarcely spoken the words when he realised that it was the wrong approach. The vice-consul bristled.

'Help? My dear fellow, the whole thing's been handled by me, and I can assure you everything's in order.'

'I'm quite sure of that, but you see, Ingram was on the staff, so the Office thought one of us ought to be around. As a matter of fact, I'm quite curious to know how these affairs are dealt with when the police force is as thin on the ground as it is here. It's a pretty peaceful place. isn't it?'

'You're right about the police, of course. They're split between the town lot, the tourist police and the gendarmerie, and it takes a bit of know-how to get action, although I've got them all taped now. You've no idea the problems I have with hippies and addicts, as well as spots of bother over the local girls. I wonder whether the Office realizes how much work we non-career consuls have to do in prime tourist areas. D'you really want to know about my job?'

'Well, yes, I do. It's part of my job to understand your problems. Particularly the procedure when a British subject's got himself into trouble. Perhaps we could have a chat, when it's convenient to you.'

'Of course, my dear fellow. Delighted. What about a stingah at six-thirty? My flat.'

'That'd be fine. I'd like to hear more about Ingram's death, too.' He noted the vice-consul's address, and accepted a lift to the Cavalieri.

## CHAPTER THREE

The Cortina drove down a wide road rising to a view of the sea and turned into the broad Kapodistriou. The vice-consul stopped in front of a handsome building in the old Corfiot

21

style. Grant thanked him, and went into the Cavalieri to collect his bag and check in.

From the window of his room the view was impressive, as Jenny had said. Although the sun had left the gardens of the Esplanade immediately below, it still shone in a golden glow on the high walls and bastions of the ancient Angevin fort that jutted out from the northern end of Garitsa Bay. Only a few miles away, beyond the straits, the mountains of Albania brooded above the narrow coastal strip which forms part of mainland Greece.

Grant dumped his holdall on the bed and asked the exchange to put him through to Miss Otfield. As the connection was made he heard her voice say something in Greek. 'It's me, Jenny. Listen. I'm going to have a drink with the V-C at half-past six. Would you like to dine with me later? I thought of the Corfu Palace. It's just down the road. Or you suggest somewhere.'

'Let's go to the old town; it's much more interesting. I know a place by the port and it's only ten minutes walk or so. Unless you want international food, the cooking's as good as you'll get. It's only the tablecloths and the waiters' clothes that are different from the plush restaurants.'

'Fine, then. About half-past seven.'

'That'll be nice ... Was she there? At the funeral, I mean.'

'Mrs Ingram? Yes, of course. But I didn't

talk to her. Shall I pick you up here?'

'No, I'll be in one of the cafés, under the arcades along the Liston. It's just opposite the cricket ground. Turn left from the hotel and you can't miss it.' She paused. 'Lucas?'

'Most people call me Luke.'

'I tried the hotel where that Greek friend of mine was staying, but they said he'd checked out last Monday.'

'I see. Right then, I'll see you on the Liston.'

He took a shower, changed, and lay down for half an hour, thinking.

\* \* \*

The previous evening Sankey had taken Grant out to dinner at his club and briefed him in greater detail than had been possible in C.I.'s office. When Grant had asked what use could be put to Katastari's information, however spectacular, if the Greeks could not be told about it, Sankey smiled. 'It's like this,' he said. 'If Roger had uncovered some Soviet conspiracy involving Greek nationals the information would be passed by my Athens liaison to Greek intelligence, without of course any mention of either Ingram or Katastari. We'd have to invent some story about the source of the information.'

'They probably wouldn't believe you.'

'That's their look-out. We'd have done our best to help them. Incidentally, as far as we

23

can make out from Athens sources, Katastari hasn't returned there since Ingram's death, which may of course mean the Soviets have collared him.'

'What d'you think he was trying to tell Ingram about?'

'Jenny Otfield will fill you in on recent Albanian history, but broadly it's like this. As you know, the Chinese have done a lot for Albania, chiefly to spite the Russians, but like everyone else they find the regime devious and difficult to handle, and the relationship doesn't seem as cordial as it was. When some reporter, before Chou-en-lai's death, asked the old boy what would happen if the Soviets threatened Albania—would the Chinese offer help?— Chou replied with an old Chinese proverb: Distant waters cannot quench fire.'

'That was explicit enough, I'd say.'

'It certainly got the Soviets thinking, and since then the country's been full of Russian spies and saboteurs, if you can believe the Albanian leaders. But it can't be easy for the KGB, because the Segurimi, Hoxha's secret police, whose leaders were all Russian trained when relations with the USSR were better, are very efficient and absolutely ruthless. And of course Albania is protected from direct Soviet infiltration by Yugoslavia and Greece. On the other hand—just to make things more complicated—both Yugoslavia and Greece lay claim to parts of Albania.'

'What, still?' asked Grant in surprise.

'Balkan people have long memories. The Albanian Government tried to stamp out all sectarian aspirations by punishing the use of other languages and abolishing wholesale all religious institutions, closing churches, mosques, monasteries and schools. Mehmet Shehu declared proudly that Albania had become the first godless state in the world. This was done as part of the cultural revolution introduced by Hoxha in imitation of Mao Tse Tung. But although the business of suppression and prescription was carried out with barbarous savagery—only in Uganda and Cambodia has there been anything like it—it didn't work. Religious festivals, both Moslem and Christian, are still observed underground, because after all the people are traditionally devout believers, one way or the other, and they don't quite see *Das Kapital* taking the place of the Koran or the Bible. Apparently— so Ingram told me—whenever there's a saint's day or a Moslem feast of some kind it's surprising what an increase there is in absenteeism, in spite of the harsh penalties incurred. And although they are risking their lives the priests and mullahs get around. It's because the cultural revolution didn't work that the Government, a few years ago, banished hundreds of writers and intellectuals to the labour camps and collective farms. Then they slashed the salaries of all officials, including political commissars, and raised the wages of the farm workers by fifty per cent. But all that did was to produce a disgruntled middle class and give the workers more money for drink and more time to plot sedition. There seems little doubt that the whole country is seething with discontent, and it's only the Segurimi that stops the pot from boiling over.'

'Yes, the Segurimi,' said Grant thoughtfully. 'By all accounts they're not nice people to know. One of the least of their tortures is to shave a man's—or woman's—head, tie their hands and leave them in a small hot cell fairly buzzing with fleas ... But if the Russians did succeed in upsetting the Shehu/Hozha regime, what would they get out of it? After all, Albania is pint-sized. Is it just a matter of prestige?'

'They want a naval base on the Adriatic. They used to have the run of the Albanian base at Saseno, but even before they broke off relations with Tirana they'd had to withdraw their subs and other naval vessels from there. In recent years, with the explosive growth of the Soviet Navy, the idea of getting Saseno back, or being allowed to build a bigger and better base, fairly makes Kremlin mouths water. And of course, with Albania in the bag they'd have a perfect springboard for the infiltration of Greece and Yugoslavia, which is all part of the long-term Soviet strategy.'

'I see. I doubt, though, if a few ethnic Albanian Greeks could start a bloody revolution, even if they could be got into the country. You simply can't overthrow a ruthless dictatorship unless you've got some rallying cry strong enough to make men and women face torture and death.'

'Exactly. That's just what the double agent, Spiro Katastari, was trying to find out—just what Vlasov is planning, and is his operation only part of something much bigger? And why does he make such an odd condition for the young Greeks that Katastari has to spot for him.'

'What condition?'

'They must all be Greek Orthodox, not Catholics or Moslems. The girl will tell you more.'

Grant sat up. 'Now that is interesting. Sectarian revolts, separate but orchestrated by a secret headquarters. Vlasov gets the Orthodox Christians working for him, someone else in Greece does the same for the Catholics, a mullah in Yugoslavia infiltrates Muslims—also probably divided into sects— and the groups these people are working on inside Albania are secret societies already, with every reason to keep their mouths shut, for fear of religious persecution.' Grant paused, frowning. 'Even then, Robert, I don't see how you can bring down a totalitarian regime just like that, with the Segurimi

27

rampant. There'd be wholesale slaughter.'

'The more slaughter, the more publicity in the world media, the more excuse for Soviet Russia to step in at the invitation of a rebel government and sort things out. It's quite possible most member countries in the UN would support them. Albania has no friends. We had a seminar on this last year, at the Castle, with Ministry of Defence experts taking part, and they made the whole thing look possible. After all, the coastline is open to infiltration by agents and *coup de main* teams put ashore by Soviet naval vessels. There could be parachute drops to breach the walls of Segurimi prisons and knock off key men, and remember, the sea is there as the escape route. The *Kirov* could be whistled up to threaten to bombard Tirana and Durazzo if the existing regime didn't throw in its hand.'

'It's a frightful risk for the Russians to take, Robert.'

'Look what they did in Afghanistan, where the vast majority of the people were against them. And they got away with it. And Saseno is a very big prize, believe me.'

'They had a common frontier with Afghanistan,' objected Grant.

'The sea could be used in the same way,' said Sankey. 'You can't close the Adriatic to Soviet warships.' He finished his brandy and pushed back his chair. 'The only way I can see any sense in what Vlasov's doing is if it's part

28

of something much bigger, that we don't know about. And that, Luke, is why Roger's death is such a tragedy.'

'Katastari may still be around, and prepared to tell Jenny what he knows.'

'If he's alive,' said Sankey.

It had been a revealing conversation, and Grant found himself looking forward to hearing Jenny's views. 'She's a bright girl,' Sankey had told him. 'She made the Junior Officers' Board last year with flying colours. Previously, she'd been Roger's head seccy.'

Grant swung his legs off the bed and stood up. Bright—oh yes, he thought. But a sad, sad girl, and he could guess why.

\*      \*      \*

The vice-consul had a pleasant flat, if a bit gloomy. From the entrance in Zambeli Street, near the Consulate, you walked up wide terrazzo stairs to a dark landing lit only by the ground-glass panels behind the ironwork of the doors. Inside, Barnard's flat was commodious and old-fashioned, with an elephant's foot umbrella stand in the hall and a living room filled with dark furniture, dominated by a grand piano which served mainly as a place to display silver-framed regimental photographs, and others in which Barnard himself shared the limelight with some large dead animal. A long-range and

29

cumbersome battery-operated radio stood on a table near the main armchair.

The V-C made Grant welcome, gave him a large whisky and water, and settled down to describe the extent of his duties and the kinds of trouble that British tourists seemed to attract. He had obviously established very friendly relations with the tourist police and the gendarmerie, and his opinion of their efficiency was quite high. 'They do things their own way, of course. Rely a lot on informers and café gossip, but once they're into a case they don't let go in a hurry.'

'Like the Ingram affair,' prompted Grant.

'Exactly. Good example. Ingram went snorkelling last Saturday morning—the water's still warm, and on the west coast it's as clean as you'd find anywhere in the Med. He left his wife in this little villa they'd rented. When he didn't turn up she got worried, went to look for him, finally got on to the local cops. Next day they found the body, very much the worse for the attentions of the lobsters which abound on that coast, but that was chiefly the face, fingers and toes. Also, of course, the—er—odd bits and pieces.' The major shuddered slightly and took a good long swallow of whisky. 'I didn't see the body, but the report was detailed enough and well drawn up. Pretty horrible, too, it sounded. The gendarmerie blokes didn't know Ingram—just seen him once or twice on the beach—but the corpse looked as if it might have been his. Fair hair, right sort of age, athletic body. But they had to get his widow to identify him. I went with her, of course. She came out looking livid pale and a bit sick, but with her head up. A plucky woman if ever I saw one. They gave her a brandy while I had a talk with the inspector. He said they'd had to keep the head covered—it wouldn't have helped if she'd seen it, because the face, well, didn't look like a face—but the torso was more or less untouched. Mrs Ingram had said yes, that was her husband. But they weren't satisfied, and asked her if he'd had any distinguishing marks on his body, and she said there was a birth-mark at the top of his right leg, in the groin. Well, that was another part they'd left covered, but they took the sheet away. She had one look before she turned her head. But it was enough. She positively identified the mark.'

'I see what you meant about their thoroughness. Poor girl! And the autopsy? When did that take place?'

'Late the following day, because they couldn't get the forensic surgeon from Athens earlier. Which was bending the rules, since bodies are supposed to be buried within twenty-four hours of discovery, or flown out of the country. It's the law here. But that report was clear, too. Death by drowning, following a heart attack.'

Grant sat up. 'Did they ask her if he'd had a

heart condition?' (There had been no mention of it in Ingram's file).

'Yes, and she said not as far as she knew. But the medics say it can happen to anyone, especially in those circumstances. Swimming in a snorkel doesn't help, and he may have tried a deep dive after some fish and gone too far. The mask was round his neck, as if he'd snatched it off.'

Grant took a sip of his drink and put the glass down. 'Why didn't she want the body sent home?'

'She said his parents had died and he had no close relatives and anyway, she knew how he loved the island, which he knew well, apparently. She thought it'd be his wish to be buried in the cemetery here.'

'So there was nothing unusual at all, as far as you could see?'

'Of course not, man, or I wouldn't have cabled the Embassy as I did. No sign of foul play, I said. I admit I was a bit surprised that at first Mrs Ingram refused to go to the cemetery, but I persuaded her. She drove there and went straight back to the villa. I think she felt the whole thing was just a formality.' The little man frowned thoughtfully. 'She'd had a very short married life to look back on. Perhaps she wished to remember her husband alive and well—and forget the images of death. And I understand.' Barnard crossed the room and picked up a photograph from the piano. It showed a woman, no longer young, but with a resolute mouth and laughter lines about the eyes. He turned back to Grant. 'My wife and I were very happy for very many years, but when she was gone I never wanted to visit her grave. This is how I want to keep her in my mind.'

There was silence for a moment. Then Grant said, 'I think I should go and see Mrs Ingram, and offer condolences from her husband's colleagues. I'd rather not, and I don't suppose she'll thank me, but as I'm here it's the least we can do. I'll see if there's anything she wants done in England.'

'Yes—yes, I suppose that's a good idea. But you'll find her very uncommunicative, Grant. It's hit her really hard, and all she wants is to be left alone so that she can come to terms with her situation. And pack up. She'll leave the villa tomorrow, and I'll put her on the plane.'

## CHAPTER FOUR

Jenny had changed into black slacks and a sweater over an apricot shirt. A heavy medallion hung between her small breasts and there were silver bracelets on her wrist. She was sitting at a table under the arches of the Liston, sipping Corfiot ginger beer and watching, like everyone else in the crowded arcades, the throng of passers-by.

All the menfolk of the town seemed to have turned out for an evening stroll under the trees of the Esplanade or to sit in the cafés, while their wives prepared supper at home. A group of handsome youths, their arms linked, went slowly by, ogling the girls, who pretended not to notice but exchanged giggling comments to keep the boys interested. There were staid older people, mostly men, talking politics or business, or engaged in family quarrels, but never missing an appreciative glance at a face or a figure, or the way a girl walked, which to experienced old eyes was just as indicative of possible pleasures. Beyond the tree-fringed road was the cricket ground, where children still chased each other in the dusk.

Jenny turned her mind resolutely from her misery and decided that the evening was to be enjoyed. After all, Roger was no more lost to her now than he had been a year ago, she told herself. She was to be squired by an attractive man—for after all, in spite of that rugged face he was quite—well, dishy, she supposed. And of course, in the Firm he was famous. He had been involved in one or two cases that had been the subject of lectures on the SIS training courses. That thwarted revolution in Bolivia, for one.

She saw him coming through the tables, tall, with a taut wiry body, his dark hair slightly greying at the temples. A suede jacket hung from his shoulders over a raw silk shirt. Jenny smiled. Here was Grant, a man used to dangerous, urgent assignments, and he was checking out a perfectly straightforward case of death by misadventure, like any village bobby. A pity. It would have been interesting to see him coping with something more vital. And it would have taken her mind off other, sadder things.

'What are you smiling at?' He was at her side, pulling out one of the padded iron chairs that the comfort-loving Corfiots like to find in Liston cafés.

'I was just thinking it seems the wrong sort of *ambiente* for a man of your reputation. It's such a peaceful island. It's only the tourists who misbehave here.'

'Somebody's been talking nonsense. I don't care for violence.' He glanced at her glass. 'What on earth's that?'

'One of the legacies of British rule, like cricket and the police force. It's ginger beer, and very good if you're thirsty. They call it *tsintsin bira*. But I'd like an ouzo now, if I may.'

'Me too.' He raised a long arm, and rather to Jenny's surprise a waiter came up at once, took the order and hurried away.

'What happened with the V-C?' asked Jenny.

'As the Queen's representative in these islands he struck me as a good choice. He obviously doesn't regard consular work as just

35

a chore, as some of the non-career people do. He has good relations with the police and he certainly seems to have handled Ingram's death very competently. I liked him. If we did run into any trouble here—which God forbid, and it seems very unlikely—I think he'd help.'

She looked away. 'And the cause of death, was that quite clear?'

'Quite clear. Ingram had a heart attack in the water and drowned.' Grant saw the startled look on her face and went on, 'It can happen to an apparently healthy man in the prime of life, Jenny. He wouldn't have suffered at all.'

'Is it so obvious what he meant to me?' she asked in a low voice.

'Well, perhaps. And it would have been strange if he wasn't fond of you, too,' he added awkwardly.

'I thought he was. After Roger was transferred he wrote once or twice and we arranged to meet in London when I went home on leave. Then nothing—until I saw the notice in *The Times*. It was a shock.' The ouzo had arrived, and she poured water into the colourless liquid and watched it cloud through. 'And Clare saw his body?'

'Yes.' He must spare her the details. 'She had no doubts at all.'

'I see. So it's quite straightforward, as we expected. All we have to do now is find out what happened to Spiro. I told you he'd left his hotel on Monday.'

'Did the reception clerk say he'd checked out personally? It could have been someone else, couldn't it?'

'Yes, I suppose so.' Her face showed awakening interest. 'You mean, anyone could have gone to the hotel, said he was a friend of Spiro's, paid the bill and collected his luggage. But what about his passport? That would have been deposited with the reception.'

'Good point. If what you've just said did happen, the reception clerk should in theory have refused to hand over the passport without specific authorization from the holder. Could you check on that, Jenny? Ring up from here, say you're a friend — use a false name—and ask if his passport's still there?'

'OK.' She picked up her handbag and disappeared into the café.

It was some time before she returned, and Grant was idly watching two pretty Greek girls, slim as naiads, who had just finished enormous slices of sticky cake and were asking their escorts for more, when Jenny slid back into her chair and picked up her glass.

Her eyes were sparkling with excitement. 'The clerk says the gentleman who came for the luggage—and he paid the bill, too—said Mr Katastari would be calling for the passport. But he hasn't turned up, and the clerk said would I please tell him that the passport would have to be sent to the police if he didn't fetch it. I said I would. He didn't ask my name.'

'Now we're getting somewhere. When Ingram sent that message to your head of station what did he say Spiro was going to do?'

'Spiro had written that he'd be arriving in Corfu on Thursday, would put up at the Calypso and ring Roger at the villa to arrange where they'd meet, and when. You know the rest of Spiro's letter—that he had something very important that he could only tell to Roger?'

'Yes. That must have been painful for you.'

'It was. I was getting along with Spiro very well, or so I thought.'

'I'd like to hear more about Spiro later. But let's see what we've got. Spiro *does* come to Corfu, and he does put up at the Calypso. But we don't know if he telephoned to Ingram or arranged a rendezvous. That's what we've got to find out from Mrs Ingram tomorrow if we can. D'you want more ouzo, or shall we leave it for the restaurant?'

'Leave it for Averof's. Don't expect too much, Luke. It's just a taverna.'

'Oh Lord, not one of those places where there's a phony folk-lore atmosphere and they make all the tourists dance?'

'Not this one. You go to Avero's to eat and drink.'

Nikolai Vlasov was comfortably sitting on the vine-covered terrace of his rented villa, twenty kilometres by road from Corfu town and at the water's edge of a secluded bay. There was a glass of iced vodka and a plate of *zakuski* on the table by his side, and he was just selecting a caviar canape when his assistant came out of the house-door with a shorthand pad in his hand. 'Andreas has just called by radio, comrade major.'

'What's he say?'

'The clerk at the Calypso has told him that the woman rang again at seven-thirty, asking if Spiro's passport was still held by the reception. She was told it was, and Spiro would have to pick it up personally, and as soon as possible. If not, the police would be informed.' The young officer smiled. 'Spiro's hardly in a position to do that, is he, comrade?'

'As you say, Sasha. But we don't want the police alerted. Tell Andreas to get the clerk to remove the passport when he has a chance and forge Spiro's signature on a receipt. He can tell the management Katastari called, signed for his passport, and left. That'll stop that hole. The other thing's more complicated. Obviously it's SIS on the trail of their lost agent. Get Andreas to make enquiries at the hotels—no, it'd take all night. Wait a moment. Did Andreas say if the woman spoke Greek?'

'Yes, comrade. Very fluently, the manager said, but with a foreign accent.'

'Aha. Then it might be Jennifer Otfield. That would fit. They wouldn't want to send a senior officer from the Athens station, but they might send Otfield, whose Greek is said to be very good, to have a sniff round. After all, she worked for Ingram at one time. Yes, get him to try the main hotels and see if she's arrived. Not the Corfu Palace or the Hilton—they're too expensive for the penny-pinching British. The Suisse, Astron, Cavalieri; the Excelsior perhaps—that sort of price bracket, and Andreas should try those to start with and go down the scale, with any others he can think of. If Otfield is in Corfu I want to know— tonight, make that clear—where she's staying and if possible the number of her room. But impress it on Andreas that his enquiries mustn't attract attention. The last thing I want is that the police should get suspicious at this stage; I want them to continue in blissful ignorance until it's too late.' Vlasov smiled thinly. 'I'm sorry, Sasha, but this is urgent, and it can't he transmitted in clear speech. Draft it out now, bring it for me to see and then you'll have to encode it and get it on the air to Andreas, using the emergency procedure. They can take your dinner in to you while you're working.'

Vlasov drew the vodka bottle from its ice-bucket and poured himself another glass. It was maddening to have to depend on half-trained Greek agents for the leg-work. In Athens he would have been able to whistle up airport lists, hotel guest lists—how did the British put it?—at the drop of a hat, and there would have been trained teams of surveillance men who could be mobilized by a phone call. But the KGB had no 'legal' residency in Corfu—there'd never been any need for one—and the illegals were concerned with personality targets. His chief at the Athens Embassy, Colonel Andreev, had insisted that the illegals were not to be used for the *Greek Fire* operation. He had said the Greeks, and especially the Corfiots, talked too easily when anything aroused their endless curiosity. If the secrecy of the Corfu part of the operation was to be kept it must be because Vlasov's administrative organization on the island was too small to be noticed. He could have one Russian assistant and up to half a dozen expendable Greek operatives recruited by him personally, and that was it. He could have more money if necessary, but no more men.

And the near-disaster of the previous weekend, when the whole operation had seemed to be in jeopardy, had not altered Andreev's attitude.

Vlasov stretched his legs luxuriously. That interview with the colonel in Athens the day before had gone off quite well, and he had hurried away to his flat to change into the clothes and identity of Felipe Rossi, rich Italian playboy, and drive to Patras for the return trip to Corfu in his motor-cruiser. It was good to get away from Andreev's baleful presence. Like the other westernized young

KGB officers in the legal residency, Vlasov hated the colonel, who had been trained by Beria and took pleasure in terrorizing his staff.

In fact, the meeting in the *referentura* had been a picnic compared with that earlier, ghastly interview, when Andreev had first learned that Spiro was double-crossing. He had turned his ice-cold eyes on Vlasov and said, in his most menacing voice, 'I hope what you tell me is true, Nikolai Viktorich, and that Katastari knows nothing of Operation *Greek Fire*. Nevertheless, he might have made an inspired guess, and it strikes me as a remarkable coincidence that he plans to meet Ingram in Corfu, of all places. You will make sure that Katastari is taken before he can meet Ingram, and you will find out from him exactly what he has already revealed. You may use extreme pressure on him. Don't let there be any mistake about this, comrade.'

But there *had* been a mistake. (It made Vlasov sweat even to think of it). He had not dared tell his chief that the kidnap team had failed to trace Spiro at his Athens flat or any of his usual haunts. Instead, Vlasov had flown to Corfu to tackle the problem at first-hand, using his own Greek operatives. And he had triumphed. Andreev might call it wriggling out of the jam, but he had effectively stopped the mouths of both Katastari and Ingram, and Operation *Greek Fire* had not been imperilled.

He lit a long Russian cigarette and drew on

it, savouring the feeling of relief. With epicurean care he spread a piece of fresh toast with butter and caviar, squeezed lemon juice over it, and held it in his left hand while he knocked back the glass of iced vodka. Then he popped the *zakuska* into his mouth and munched contentedly.

\*       \*       \*

Grant and Jenny left the café under the arches and walked out into the lively streets. It was nearly eight o'clock, but the shops were all doing a brisk business and the pedestrian precincts were full of people strolling to the bouzouki music that issued from every record shop. A delicious smell of charcoal and roasting meat came from a small restaurant at the top of Nikiforou Theotoki, and Grant stopped. 'What about that one? I'm hungry.'

'We're going to Avery's,' said Jenny firmly. 'They know me there, and it makes all the difference.'

The tourist shops, with their tinsel jewellery and garish, hastily-made clothes, gave way to the brief calm of a square, flanked by a church with a tall illuminated spire. Candle-light flickered in the windows. Skilfully concealed lights accented the beauty of the old Venetian buildings which had housed merchants and bankers long before Italy had been united as a nation.

'We turn off here,' said Jenny, and they left N. Theotoki through a narrow passage into a quiet little square where a small crumbling chapel appeared to be devoting itself mainly to the support of a rogue bougainvillaea, whose magenta flowers tumbled from the belfry. A few twisting alleys brought them to an archway leading to the old port. A buzz of voices and the clatter of plates and cutlery broke the silence of the half-deserted street. They passed plate glass windows behind which people were sitting eating under the merciless glare of the harsh strip lighting. Grant's heart sank, but Jenny drew him round the corner into a courtyard with a baroque fountain framed in ancient stonework at the far end. Tables took up the space beneath a striped awning stretched from wall to wall, and they were already fully occupied.

Seeing Jenny, a fat little waiter with a heavy black moustache flung his arms wide and shouted a greeting. A boy came running from the restaurant carrying a table, legs first, high in the air. There was a scraping of chairs as diners were crowded together to make room for it, but nobody seemed to mind. The waiter, still talking to Jenny, whisked a fresh cloth over the stained table top, snapped his fingers to a boy with a tray of glasses, and took a pencil from behind his ear and a pad from his apron pocket.

'Retsina,' said Jenny, 'while we decide what

we're going to eat. Or perhaps you don't like it?'

'I'll try anything,' said Grant cheerfully. 'Though I don't promise to stick with it. What are we going to eat?'

'The Greeks are chaotic in their eating habits,' explained Jenny. 'But it works out very well if you like experimenting. They put a number of dishes on the table at once, and everyone dips into each other's. That's quite fun.' She glanced at Grant to gauge his reaction. 'You can ask for a half portion if you like. But it's safer not to mention hot dishes together with the first course, or they may bring everything at once and you have to race through the starters while you watch your favourite hot dish congealing on the table. Oh good, here's the wine.'

The little boy had come back with a bottle of cold dry retsina and was filling their glasses. The waiter rushed up with plates and cutlery, took the girl's order and disappeared. There was a gabble of conversation, mostly Greek, with an admixture of every language in Europe from the crews of the yachts anchored in the port close by, and from the tourists who had ventured out from the hotels.

Jenny took a quick look at Grant to see if he was enjoying himself. He was. He was raising a full glass of wine. 'To your bright eyes, Jenny.'

And they were bright. She, too, was enjoying herself. 'It's nice to be with you,

45

Luke. You're married, of course?'

'No. Should I be?'

'Nice men usually are,' she said, with a trace of bitterness. Then she shifted her ground quickly. 'Anyhow, I'm not sure that I'd envy your wife, sitting quietly at home while you go off to some remote part of the world and get into another scrape.'

Grant finished his glass of retsina. 'I like this stuff. It's pleasant, and suits the climate. Let's have some more.' While he refilled Jenny's glass he looked at her quizzically. 'I told you. You've got the wrong idea about my life. Most of the time I'm sitting at my desk. I hate violence.'

'It just seems to come your way,' said Jenny smiling.

'Well, I've been in one or two what you slightingly called scrapes in recent years, but they're exceptional. I prefer peace. But look who's talking. You're launched on a career in SIS, up to all kinds of skulduggery, working for the most devious bunch of men I know.' He added hastily, 'And women.'

'They may be devious,' she flashed indignantly, 'but you must agree they're dedicated. And your colleagues.'

'Oh I give you that. And I'll agree we're often very successful. But that's because we aren't hidebound by rules, like the CIA and the KGB. We're just gifted amateurs.'

'What a horribly superior remark! Do you

realize how many months of training I've gone through, for a start?'

'In the KGB it'd have been years. Here comes the food.'

The taramasalata was served with thick hunks of bread, crisp and coarse, and there was a bowl of Greek salad—tomatoes, cucumber and olives with slices of white feta cheese. It was delicious, and for a time they both ate without speaking. Grant called for more retsina. 'Tell me about Katastari,' he invited.

'He's tall and fair—some Greeks are—and is married with two children. Which didn't stop him from making a pass at me when he had the chance. Without success.'

'He seems to have good taste, anyway.'

'He'd make a pass at any girl he found himself alone with. It's a way young Greeks have, at least as far as foreign birds are concerned. But he's bright, and quite nice, really. Roger had trained him in personal security, coding and report drafting—he was a good photographer already, which was fortunate, because training takes a lot of sessions—and while I've been running him he's scarcely made a mistake.' She was keeping her voice down, although with the noise of plates and the polyglot chatter all around there was hardly any need.

'And he worked for you as willingly as he did for Roger?'

'No, of course not. Greeks don't like taking orders from women. And as you know, the moment he got hold of something really important he went over my head to Roger. That stung, Luke. It still does.'

'If it had been anyone else but Roger you mightn't have minded so much,' hazarded Grant.

'Of course not. There's no need to be subtle, Luke. It's obvious that I didn't want Roger to think I wasn't up to the job. It was he who'd taught me fieldwork in Greece and— and I was very fond of him.' She glanced at Grant's face, then quickly away. 'You may as well know. He never asked me to marry him, but he might've done if he hadn't met Clare. Or so I like to think. And now let's talk of something else.' She studied the menu, face slightly flushed, chin up, the small vulnerable mouth set.

'Choose something you'd like. I'm sure I shall too.'

'OK then. Let's have a pastisada. It's a relic of the Venetian occupation, I suppose—spiced veal on a bed of macaroni. Will the retsina do, or do you want to try another wine—the demestica, perhaps?'

'No. And I like Italian dishes.' The little waiter took the order and rushed away. 'He never seems to stop running. What d'you think has happened to Spiro, Jenny?'

'Your guess is as good as mine. At the worst,

the KGB may have suspected him, followed him here, and when they found he was going to meet Roger—collared him. If so, I don't like to think what's happening to him now. As for Roger, if he didn't die naturally it must have been the KGB. Perhaps they got him at the same time as Spiro. They have an injection that simulates death from a heart attack, haven't they?'

'Yes. They've used it before. But why kill him?'

'Perhaps he'd already met Spiro and de-briefed him before the KGB men got there. If so, I suppose they'd have to kill him, and make it seem natural.'

She was talking without any sign of emotion now. 'There's a sort of convention—isn't there?—that espionage services don't kill off each other's officers, for fear of reprisals. And Vlasov wouldn't want to alert the Greek police to what he's doing here. And that's what would happen if a British diplomat was found to have been murdered.'

The pastisada was excellent, and both ate for some time without reverting to the business that had brought them together. Then Grant said, 'And what is he doing? Vlasov, I mean.'

'What did they tell you in London?'

'Only that Spiro was talent-spotting for Vlasov, fingering Greeks with Albanian connections.'

'Well, that's it. Spiro is a very active journalist, for one of the big Athens dailies, and he gets round a lot, writing both news and feature stories. When he's spotted someone he thinks would work for the Russians, either for ideological reasons or cash, he tells Vlasov. And me. So I've compiled quite a list of young men—'

'No women? And are they all young?'

'All young men, Greek Orthodox and unmarried, and they have to be very fit. Some are Communists, undeclared of course, but not all. Spiro has to get to know them very well, as you can imagine, before he puts forward their names, but after that he is ordered to have no further dealings with them.'

'That must lead to some awkward situations. And isn't he inquisitive?'

'As a chimp, but he's afraid of Vlasov. He only broke the rule once, and then it was a chance encounter. He was over here, in Corfu, following up some news story down in the port area, when he ran into a man called Bulgareos whom he'd spotted for Vlasov. The man threw his arms round Spiro and insisted they should go into one of the harbour bars. He paid for the first round from a roll of hundred drachma notes, and Spiro got curious and couldn't resist plying him with more ouzo and trying to get him to talk. He didn't at first, but looked very sly and said he'd been given good work, well paid. Spiro asked what it was, and Bulgareos smiled and laid a finger alongside his nose, to show it was secret. So Spiro said, 'Drugs, I suppose,' in a very bored voice—I told you he was bright—and the man looked affronted and said it was something quite different. He had been specially selected for a very difficult job, and had spent a week on Paxos, learning all about it.'

'Paxos? That's the little island south of Corfu, isn't it?'

'Yes. So Spiro said he didn't know of any trade schools on Paxos, which as you say is very small and almost covered with olive groves. And the other Greek laughed and said it was a special kind of trade, and he and the trainer had spent the week together in an empty house right on the edge of the cliffs. Then he shut up, looking frightened, and wouldn't say any more. Spiro had to swear he wouldn't tell a soul. He was full of it when I met him back in Athens.'

'Spy training?' conjectured Grant. 'For the infiltration of Albania?'

'Spiro was certain that was it, and it made him more curious than ever. It does seem the obvious explanation. You just can't teach an agent security or coding or secret writing at occasional meetings; you've got to get him alone, away from distractions, and teach him ten hours a day. All the more so if he's a Greek; you have to practically brainwash them first, before you can instill even elementary ideas of security tradecraft into them.'

'It certainly sounds like a training school,' said Grant. 'And you think Spiro ferreted around until he found what Vlasov was up to?'

'Yes. And he was determined to show Roger how clever he'd been. He's the sort of man who needs praise all the time, and mine,' she added with a wry smile, 'wasn't enough.'

'And perhaps, to earn Ingram's praise, he risked his life,' said Grant thoughtfully. 'I wonder how on earth he could have found out the solution, if he was only a talent-spotter.'

'I've puzzled over that a lot, and all I can think of is that Vlasov's plans were maturing, and he had to get more active collaboration from Spiro. Good and reliable Greek agents aren't all that easy to recruit, as we know too well.' She laughed suddenly. 'And don't forget that Spiro had been trained by Roger, so naturally he was a good worker . . . But there may have been another reason.'

'And that is . . . ?' Grant reached for the bottle and refilled her glass.

'Spiro comes from this island. (Half the male Corfiots are named Spiridion). He knows it like the back of his hand. Now if the KGB were planning some new infiltration of Greek agents into Albania they might well decide to have a base here. The land routes across the Epirot mountains are difficult and well guarded by the Albanians. But the snag is that the suspected KGB 'diplomats' in Athens are kept under constant surveillance by the Greek counter-espionage service, and so far as we know they've never had any organization in Corfu. If they come here, they come as tourists, with false passports. Someone like Spiro might be very useful.'

Grant ordered coffee and brandy and lit a cigar. 'I'm glad you told me all this, Jenny. We'll hope to find out more tomorrow from Mrs Ingram. If Spiro went to the villa she must have met him. And I also want to know exactly how Ingram disappeared.'

*     *     *

Vlasov was standing on his terrace, watching the moon rise over the Albanian mountains, when the telephone rang. He went indoors to the ground-floor extension. A voice queried, 'Signor Rossi?'

'*Sono io,*' said Vlasov. '*Chi parla?*'

'It's me,' said Andreas's voice, in English. 'You asked about hotels. There are rooms at the Cavalieri, and I can recommend it.'

'Thank you. I'll let you know first thing tomorrow what I decide to do. Goodnight.' So that was where the Otfield girl was staying. Vlasov went upstairs to his study and wrote out a message in Greek: ARRANGE FOR SURVEILLANCE OF OTFIELD BY KEL., WITH CAR AVAILABLE. STAY AT BASE AND MAINTAIN RADIO CONTACT.

KEEP ME INFORMED OF OTFIELD'S MOVEMENTS AND CHECK WHETHER SHE IS WITH OTHER BRITISH PERSONNEL. IF SO, WHO? AS BEFORE, USE UTMOST DISCRETION AND INSTRUCT KEL. ACCORDINGLY.

He rang for his assistant and gave him the message. 'I've told Andreas he will get this by the first schedule tomorrow, Sasha. You'd better encode it before you go to bed and see that it is sent off promptly at six o'clock. Goodnight.'

## CHAPTER FIVE

Next morning Jenny was brisk when they met at breakfast. 'When d'you want to go to the villa?' she asked, pouring coffee.

'As soon as we can get away, I think. Did you sleep well?'

'Marvellously. If we hire a car it'll take us less than half an hour. It's not far across the island, but there's a stretch of bad road, according to Roger's sketch map.'

'When did he send you that?'

'Not me. The station. When he wrote to say he'd be staying with Clare in Corfu. Have you got plenty of money?'

'In traveller's cheques, yes, but I'm glad you reminded me. I'd better get hold of a few thousand drachs in case Mrs Ingram needs anything. Will the banks be open?'

'From eight-thirty, I think. We'll probably have to pay a deposit on the car, though there is a place where they waive it if they think you look respectable.'

'I've got an American Express card.'

'That's easy, then. We'll need your passport and driving licence, and you'd better have full insurance as well as third party, which is obligatory, of course.'

'What a wonderful secretary you must have been before your elevation to higher rank!'

'I'm an officer now, and don't you forget it.' She smiled at him, then turned her attention to the crisp rolls and a pot of honey.

She is getting over the shock, thought Grant. It would be a shame to set her back again. 'Listen, Jenny,' he said. 'There's no need for you to come to the villa. It might be a bit painful for you, because I've got to ask a lot of questions,'

'Thanks, but I'll come with you,' she said quickly, and Grant wondered how much of her decision was due to a sense of duty to 'The Firm' and how much to a very feminine desire to see for the first time the woman who had succeeded in capturing Roger Ingram.

'OK. We'll do better as a team. What sort of cars do they have?'

'Small Fiats and Datsuns, and some larger cars. Shall I get a Fiat 124? If they've got one available?'

'Yes, that'd do nicely. If there's nothing we can do for Clare Ingram and there's no trace of Spiro I'll try to get a passage home this evening. But there's no desperate hurry, so let's leave that until we get back.'

Half an hour later they had hired the Fiat and Grant was driving round the port through a shoal of mopeds ridden by a group of tourists. He turned away from the sea on a broad road that rose curving through the low hills.

She pulled a scrap of paper from her shirt pocket. 'Roger explained the route, in case anyone had to contact him from the station. We follow the Ermones road and branch off to the left—I'll show you where —on a little track which ends in the hamlet of Vatos, but we turn off again before we reach it.'

The Ermones road ran across a wide valley. Grant drove more slowly, and they could hear the tinkling of goat bells and the sound of singing as a woman in black followed her straggling herd through the aromatic brush, chanting in a cracked harsh voice some song as old as the ancient trees. The goats pushed slowly through the cystus and myrtles, browsing on what they fancied.

'Turn left here.' The unfinished road twisted steeply uphill. One fork ended in the hamlet of Vatos, the other bent leftwards to run along the crest of the hill towards Pelekas.

After a few hundred yards a rough track led down a small valley. 'The villa must be down here,' said Jenny.

'We'll drive the car out of sight of the road and continue on foot.'

They walked down the narrow valley. The sunlight filtered through the silvery foliage of the olives on to the tiny wild flowers of autumn. The ancient tree trunks twisted against the flickering background like the pattern on an early tapestry.

'Look,' said Jenny suddenly, 'that must be the house.' She pointed up the slope on their right. A narrow path, flanked by a line of shaky-looking telephone poles, led up towards an ancient tiled roof glimpsed through the trees, and stopped at the vinecovered terrace of a small house. The view over the hillside to the sea far below must be enchanting, thought Grant, but the shutters were closed. The stone slabs of the terrace had been swept clear of leaves, and a besom stood against the circular parapet of an ancient well. The place was completely quiet except for the hum of insects and the whirring of the few cicadas which had survived the summer. Then they heard the tapping of a typewriter inside the house.

'She's there,' said Grant. 'That's something.' He crossed the flagged terrace and knocked on the door between the shuttered windows.

They heard the scrape of chair legs and the door was opened. Clare Ingram stood on the threshold, and she seemed startled. It was the first time Grant had seen her face, and for a moment he was held by its beauty.

Jenny thought, generously, you could hardly blame Roger. She was lovely, with the pale gold hair drawn back in to a knot, large grey eyes, delicate high cheek-bones and the graceful set of her head above the russet shirt loosely buttoned over pale linen slacks. Her bare feet were thrust into sandals—and even her toe-nails were perfectly groomed. Beautiful, thought Jenny, but hard as a gemstone. Then she felt ashamed. This woman had lost Roger, just as she had.

'I saw you at the funeral, Mrs Ingram. I'm Lucas Grant, from Head Office, and this is Miss Otfield from the Embassy in Athens. We don't want to intrude at a time like this, but the Office thought I might be able to help you. Is there anything we can do?'

'Nothing, thank you.' The soft lips took on a determined line. There was a moment of hesitation. 'Perhaps you'd like a drink. Wine, ouzo, coffee?'

'Coffee, please,' said Jenny, and Grant nodded his thanks as they entered the house.

The long room, low-beamed, with islands of rush matting on the stone floor, was bare but pleasant. At the far end Clare busied herself making coffee on a tiled ledge. 'Do sit down,' she said, turning round. 'And please don't think you have to say anything ... It doesn't help. I've just got to get things sorted out in my own mind, you see, and . . .'

'Of course.' There were cane armchairs by the hearth. Grant and Jenny sat down and waited until Clare joined them with mugs of coffee.

'I'm sorry,' began Grant awkwardly, 'but there are some questions I have to ask. You see, the Office wants a fairly detailed report.'

'Hasn't Major Barnard written that already?'

'There are still a few things that aren't clear. Perhaps you could tell us the sequence of events last Saturday.'

She shrugged her shoulders. 'Roger said he was going snorkelling last Saturday morning, off the Mirtiotissa rocks, and—'

'What time was this?'

'About half-past seven, I think. It was a warm, lovely day, and he said he might take a snack of lunch at Glyfada and go on afterwards if there were plenty of fish around.'

'And then?' prompted Grant gently.

'He didn't return. I was busy writing letters and wasn't worried until late in the afternoon, when I walked down to Glyfada—Roger had taken our car—and an old man told me Roger had hired a boat from him. He thought he was going to take it to a cove below the monastery. I found the car parked behind the taverna and waited until dark. Then I drove back here and rang the police.' Clare's voice was devoid of expression and her face, with its flawless bone structure and smooth golden tan, showed no sign of inner feeling. Grant realised that she had told the story before, many times probably, and might in any case still be suffering from shock.

She went on wearily, 'Next day the police came. Roger's body had been washed up at the southern end of the beach—just where we used to swim, and after bathing we'd wash the salt off under the fresh water that falls from the cliffs . . .' It was as if she were trying to get away from the tensions that gripped her by talking of something that had happened before the nightmare began.

'And you tried to contact the vice-consul, I believe.'

'Yes. I knew that being Sunday the Consulate would be closed, but I had his private number. There was no reply. The police said they had taken the body to Corfu for identification and would call for me in the afternoon. They said the autopsy would be next morning. Burials are supposed to take place within twenty-four hours, so they couldn't wait. They were very tactful and kind.' She looked up. 'I suppose you've already talked to the police?'

'No. Only the V-C, who told me you were very brave and gave the police a positive identification of the body. That was difficult, especially since—' He stopped, embarrassed.

'There's no need to be mealy-mouthed, Mr Grant. Most of Roger's face had gone, they said, but I recognized him by the birth-mark. It was—' Clare stopped and glanced at Jenny, who had started, and was sitting up very straight, white-faced. 'I'm sorry, Miss Otfield. I suppose you knew my husband when he was posted in Athens?'

Jenny nodded.

'Well, he had a distinctive birthmark, but you wouldn't have seen it even when he wore bathing trunks. It was high up in the groin—I have to explain this, because that's how I knew for certain it was Roger. There could be no mistake whatever, and that's what I told them. And now, I hope you're satisfied, Mr Grant. All this is rather painful both for me and Miss Otfield.'

'Of course, and I'm sorry to have had to ask these questions. There's only one other thing. Did a man come to see Roger that morning— Saturday, that is?'

The grey eyes widened. 'A man? No. What sort of man?'

'A Greek. Quite young. His name is Katastari, Spiro Katastari. Didn't Roger tell you that he might be coming to the villa?'

For a moment the grey eyes regarded him questioningly. Then she said firmly, 'No. I've never heard that name.'

As they went down the path Grant heard a twig snap in the bushes to one side. He stopped to light a cigarette, and through his cupped hands looked closely at the place the sound had come from. But there was no movement; it might after all have been a bird. Neither spoke as they walked to where Grant had parked the car.

He drove back up the track to the road, passing a small, light blue Fiat parked under the trees. It was empty, and Grant looked at it speculatively. Jenny was unusually silent, and he glanced at her face. She was frowning slightly, intent on working out some problem. After they had driven a little way she said suddenly, 'Stop for a bit, Luke. I've got to talk to you.' He drew in to the side and switched off the engine. Then he turned to the girl.

'Before you tell me what's on your mind, just pretend to be admiring the view. I have a feeling we're being followed.'

There was the sound of a car approaching, and a moment later the blue Fiat came into view. It was in low gear, because the ascent was fairly steep, and they could distinctly hear the change in note as the driver, seeing the other car, momentarily took his foot off the throttle. Then he accelerated again and went past without giving them a glance.

'That's interesting,' said Grant. 'It could be a coincidence, but I had a suspicion we were being watched when we were at the villa. We'll check if I'm right in a minute. Now tell me.'

'Luke,' Jenny burst out. 'That body wasn't

Roger's. He may be *alive*.' She was trembling with excitement. 'We've got to find him.'

Grant was staring at her flushed face. 'What was it? The identification? I thought you seemed surprised.'

'Yes, of course it was. Roger has no birthmarks.'

'But Jenny—she said it was—er—on the groin, where you couldn't see it if he was wearing bathing trunks.'

'Oh for God's sake, must I spell it out? I'd have thought you'd have guessed already. We were lovers, Luke. And we made love under trees and on lonely beaches, and with the sun streaming in through the window of my flat in Athens. I know every bit of his body, and he hasn't got a birthmark in his groin or anywhere else.' Her eyes were wide, and dark with remembered delight. She smiled at Grant suddenly and put out a hand to touch his with a fleeting gesture, not a caress but an appeal for understanding. 'Don't look embarrassed, Luke. I had to explain, and I'm not the least ashamed. I was in love with him, and he with me—as I thought. It wasn't just a casual affair. But I don't understand . . . Why should Clare pretend Roger had that mark on him? Why did she have to lie?'

'There's only one explanation I can think of always provided you're right—'

'I am right,' said Jenny fiercely.

'Then the body found on the beach was

someone else's, and Clare is under duress. She was forced into identifying it as Roger's. Blackmailed, if you like. But the object, on somebody's part, is to cover up the fact that Ingram is alive. The scheme was plain sailing until you appeared. You remember the sudden look Clare gave you when she mentioned the birthmark? She knew you must have known Roger well, but not how well, I suppose. She had to risk it because she'd guess that the V-C had told me about the mark, so—'

'Then you knew about it yesterday! Why on earth didn't you tell me? We've wasted so much time.'

'Oh Jenny, isn't it obvious? I just didn't want to distress you further, when you were already so unhappy.'

She was touched. 'That was kind. But what does it all mean? Whose body is it?'

'Could it have been Spiro's?'

'*Spiro*'s? Well, yes, I suppose it could, if there was no face to be recognized. He was fair and fair-skinned, and about the same age as Roger. In fact, he used to boast he could pass as an Englishman. Poor Spiro! He didn't realize how that might happen to prove true.' She saw Grant hesitating, and gave a nervous laugh. 'You're trying to find out if I ever slept with Spiro, so that I can confirm whether he had a birthmark. Well, I'm sorry, but I can't oblige you. I told you, that pass he made at me got him nowhere. To tell you the truth, I'm not

64

promiscuous.' She stopped laughing. 'But where is Roger?'

'As I see it, the KGB—it must have been the KGB; it doesn't make sense otherwise—captured both Ingram and Katastari *after* they'd met, that is after Ingram had received whatever important information the agent had to give him. Spiro was killed, or died naturally, but they held Ingram. So, to prevent him from reporting what he'd learned from Spiro and to keep a hold on his wife, they staged the exchange of bodies. They could then force Mrs Ingram to identify the body as her husband's, but there was the chance that one of the police or coastguards knew Ingram by sight, so—they took steps to make the face unrecognizable. I'm afraid it wasn't just the rocks and the crabs that caused the damage.'

Jenny shivered. 'It's so brutal and inhuman.'

'They've done much worse things than that, as you know, and they'd think it just a question of technique: it was essential to let Spiro disappear quietly, leaving them with an SIS officer in their hands.'

Jenny jerked round. 'You mean they may be torturing Roger to find out what he knows? Is that what you mean?'

'No,' said Grant, with misgivings. 'I think they'll keep him somewhere until they can get him on to a Soviet plane, and that means the mainland.'

'No, it doesn't,' said Jenny. 'It could be a

Soviet ship. Their cruise liners call at Corfu. Are you sure they won't torture him?'

'I think it's unlikely. He's a big prize, a medium-rank SIS officer, and a very intelligent one, and they'd want to get a great deal of information out of him. Physical torture doesn't help much for that kind of in-depth interrogation. It's effective, sometimes, for eliciting a single fact or two, like someone's name or address, but not for a job that might take six months. And it would probably be worth their while to wait, in any case, until they can bring Clare to join him. She'd be an additional means of putting pressure on him. I'm sorry to talk like this, but it's best to face up to the situation.'

Jenny shook herself. 'We've got to stop it, Luke. What do we do?'

'I believe there is something we might try, here and now. Are you prepared for a little violence?'

'Of course I am,' said Jenny stoutly.

'And can you use a gun—a revolver or automatic?'

'Yes. I've done the course. 89 per cent accuracy, too.' She looked at him frowning. 'But I haven't got one with me. Have you?'

'No, but I might just possibly be able to get one. If I do, I want to be sure you'll do exactly as I say. It's your only chance of helping to find where Roger is.'

'OK.'

'Right. Listen, then. If I hand you a gun, and say something dramatic like 'Shoot him if he moves an inch', it will of course be just for effect. I don't expect you to shoot anyone, but to be effective, the action must be right. It's only a possibility, as I said, but if it does happen you will hold the gun in both hands, you will be seen to take the safety-catch off, and you will point at the target's stomach—not the head—and keep five feet away. Not less, in case he tries to jump you, but not much more. Some people think they can take a risk if the gun appears some way away. Have you got all that?'

She nodded.

'OK, then. 'Two more things. One, you will put on as fierce an expression as your pretty face can manage, and two, keep your mouth closed to stop your lips trembling. All understood?'

'Yes,' said Jenny promptly. She couldn't see Grant's expression, but the man's whole personality seemed to have changed. Arguing with him now would be quite useless.

'One more thing. You will on no account pull the trigger. Now, our plan of action. The fact that we know Clare is acting under duress, and by the KGB—I think we can assume that—convinces me that the man in the blue Fiat is trailing us and that he'll have been told to do so unobtrusively. There'd be no point in arousing our suspicions deliberately. We'll try to capture him and find out what he can tell us. He's probably a Greek and may be really tough, but perhaps not fully trained. He's somewhere up the road, probably waiting for us to pass so that he can follow. That's when we'll try to nab him. And Jenny—'

'Yes.'

'I don't like frightening people, but it may be our best immediate way of finding out where Roger is. Clare is useless to us; she'd be afraid that if she helped us they'd kill Roger. The police won't help us either at this stage, since we're only speculating, after all. But we have to act *now*, before the KGB can have an inkling that we suspect them of being involved. You're quite sure you'll go along with my plan?'

'Of course I am, Luke. But hadn't you better tell me what it is?'

\*　　　\*　　　\*

Nearly a quarter of a mile further on there was a rough patch of grass at the left of the road, and the blue Fiat had been driven on to it and parked among some bushes that grew out to the edge of a small ravine. A man in a black jersey and jeans was relieving himself—or so it appeared—against a tree. He turned his head for a moment as the car drove by.

At this point the road was rising quite steeply, and a few yards past the clearing

Grant allowed the engine to falter, changed up instead of down, and let in the clutch with a jerk. The engine gave an outraged snort and stalled. Grant started it again, and repeated the operation. He made a third attempt, with roaring acceleration, and the inevitable stall as he took his foot off the clutch pedal. He got out of the car, spoke to Jenny for a moment through the window, and walked back to the clearing, where the man in the black jersey was standing by the road, watching him suspiciously.

'Excuse me, sir,' said Grant, with an ingratiating smile. 'Do you speak English?'

'A little,' growled the man, his watchful look switching to Jenny, who had now appeared behind Grant.

'Oh good,' said Grant. 'I wonder if you could help me. You see, I'm used to automatic cars, and I can't get this one to start on the hill.'

'I cannot help,' said the Greek curtly. 'I am late. I go now.'

'Oh surely,' said Grant persuasively, 'you could just show me how to do it.' He was going nearer as he spoke, and the man stepped back, turning towards his car.

'Please don't drive away,' cried Grant, and ran forward as if to stop him. The man spun round. His hand flew to his belt.

Jenny was never sure afterwards exactly what happened, it was so quick. Aghast, she saw the flick knife whipped from the belt, and for a split-second, as the spring was pressed, the flash of a steel blade in the sun. But it was too late. The man's arm was paralysed by a lightning chop to the muscles, and then Grant's heavy fist hit his jaw with a solid 'clunk'. He dropped to the grass like a sack of potatoes.

Grant was rubbing his knuckles. 'Always keep them uncertain about your next move, even when they suspect you.' As he spoke he was dragging the inert body well into the bushes to a spot that was concealed from the road. He ran his hands over the clothing. 'No gun. So no need for your act after all. Pick up the knife and give it to me. Are you all right?'

'Y-yes,' she said, shivering. Her hand trembled as she handed over the wicked-looking knife. He kept it open, fingering it thoughtfully.

'Good girl. Bring the car back here, and park it so that the other Fiat can't be seen from the road at a casual glance.'

As she got into the hired car two mopeds roared past, with jeans-clad couples perched on them, waving. By the time she had placed the Fiat where he had told her Grant had the man sitting against a tree, with his belt binding his arms to the trunk. The contents of his pockets lay on the grass. Amongst them was a small transceiver, like the personal radios used by the police. Grant handed a wallet to Jenny.

'Find out his name, and look carefully at the other papers. He might be someone you heard about from Spiro.'

'What are you going to do?'

The man groaned, turning his head. Grant spoke to her softly. 'The thing is to make him feel absolutely helpless, in the hands of ruthless enemies, and then use the soft and hard treatment. He'll talk. His eyes are open now. Look grim.'

Jenny thought, this man must know where Roger is. He may have helped to torture him. Her angry scowl was genuine enough. She knelt to empty out the contents of the wallet.

Grant was standing in front of the prisoner, stropping the knife on the palm of his hand and examining the man's face. He was not more than about twenty-five, with heavy black eyebrows that almost met across the bridge of his nose, a dark face marked by smallpox or severe acne, and jet-black fuzzy hair, cut short.

'What's your name?'

The man shook his head contemptuously.

'Mehmet Kellezi,' said Jenny. 'Albanian, naturalized Greek. He's a stevedore from Piraeus.' The man glanced at the identity card in her hand and spat.

'I remember now,' continued Jenny. 'He used to be a sailor in the P & O ships, but got sacked because he knifed an officer when he was drunk. He's bluffing, by the way. His English is quite good, from his time on British ships. He left his wife and two children last year and went to live with a woman in Patras. The Athens police want him for pimping.' Jenny repeated that last sentence in Greek, to make sure the man understood.

Kellezi had started violently, and was looking up at her with an expression of complete bafflement on his face.

'His friends,' continued Jenny, 'call him Kiki.'

'And now.' said Grant, 'he's working for the Russians, but they don't seem to be paying very handsomely.' He glanced at the pile of small notes that lay on the ground. Then he took from his notecase a couple of thousand drachma notes. 'That's what they ought to pay for the work he's been doing. Like killing his old friend Spiro Katastari. The police will be itching to get their hands on him.'

'No,' shouted the man. 'It wasn't me. It was—' His mouth closed obstinately.

'Who was it, then?' asked Grant. 'If you tell me everything I might let you go and,' he added, showing the notecase in his hand, 'give you enough to make a run for it. Before the police catch up with you.'

'No,' growled Kellezi.

Grant sighed. 'Then the police. We can show them how we know you killed Katastari.'

The man's heavy face was sweating with fear, but he said stubbornly, 'You can't prove it.'

'Oh yes we can. And then there's the Athens pimping charge.'

Before the man could reply the little transceiver emitted a muted 'bleep-bleep'.

Jenny stared at the little machine, horrified. 'What now?' she whispered. 'It'll be his control, wanting a report.'

'Then he shall have one,' said Grant cheerfully. There was a second series of bleeps from the set. He knelt down quickly at Kellezi's side, put one hand on his throat to keep his head back and with the other jerked open his jacket and pointed the knife at the man's bare stomach. 'Tell him in Greek to say he has us still in sight. We've turned south towards Cavos and are stopping now and then to look at the view. He thinks we're just touring.' Again the double bleep. 'If he diverges in the least from what you tell him, nod your head, and I'll put some pressure on this.' As he spoke, with his eyes on Kellezi's, he pushed the knife slowly into the ground, then brought it up, menacingly, and held the point against the man's skin.

'OK.' As the bleeping began again the girl spoke to Kellezi in Greek, picked up the radio, switched to 'Send' and held it to his mouth.

For a moment, with his eyes on the knife that was already pricking his stomach, Kellezi hesitated. Then he began to speak. When he had finished Jenny switched back to 'Receive' and brought her head down to listen. A

73

crackling voice made some remark, and there was a sharp click.

'He said report in half an hour,' said Jenny.

'Good. Did this man say anything at all in addition to what you told him?'

'No. He's got to tell us where Roger is, Luke.'

'Yes.' Grant turned to the man, who was staring at him truculently. 'You heard her. Where is the Englishman?'

'I don't know—ugh!' He felt the knife-point stabbing at his flesh. 'I tell you I don't know. They took him away. The Russian and another.'

'How? By car?'

'No. He brought his boat into the cove below the monastery. That's where they caught them—Spiro and the other man, the Englishman. They were sitting on the rocks, talking, and the Russian brought his boat in close, as if he was going to land, and then held them up with his gun. It was all very quick, because anyone could have swum round the point and caught us.'

'So you were on the boat,' observed Grant. 'Where had you come from?'

The man hesitated for a moment, then seeing the look on Grant's face said hurriedly, 'From Patras, on Thursday night. In the Russian's cabin-cruiser. I filled the tank with gas, and brought it across to Corfu, where my job was to keep watch on Spiro. The Russian came over by plane. The following day I found out that Spiro, who was staying at the Calypso, tried twice to get through to a Paleocastritsa number, and arranged to meet someone. I told Andreas, who is the man I work for on these watching jobs, and he said he knew who it was. Spiro didn't leave Corfu that day, but on the Saturday he took a bus to Paleocastritsa. I was on the bus, too,' added Kellezi, with evident satisfaction.

'But where was the yacht?'

'That was the surprise. When I got out at Paleocastritsa the yacht was already in the bay. I saw Spiro, who was carrying a bag, hire a small motor-boat and set off towards Glyfada, so I started to follow him in a rowing boat, but I'd called Andreas by radio, and the yacht caught me up and took me aboard. We followed Spiro at a distance—although as it was Saturday there were quite a number of boats on the water, so it was unlikely Spiro would have spotted us—and we saw him anchor off Mirtiotissa beach. He put on his skin-diving suit and began to swim round the point to the little cove where the Englishman was waiting for him. They'd chosen it because you can't get there by land without a lot of climbing. The Russian took the wheel of the yacht and edged in, as I said, and caught them. It was quite simple.'

'And afterwards?'

'I don't know, exactly. Mr Rossi—that's

what he calls himself—gave me a note for the lady in the villa and I went ashore in the rowing-boat, which we'd been towing, and delivered it. They had put Spiro and the Englishman in the saloon, and I saw the yacht head out to sea, going north. That's all.'

'And what did you do then?'

'I went back by bus to Corfu and reported to Andreas.'

'Where?'

Kellezi hesitated, and Grant prodded him with the knife, painfully. He said hastily, 'He has an apartment in Bitzaru, near the new fort in the Kambielo. I don't know the number. He had nothing for me to do until this morning.' He looked up at Grant and said in a pleading voice, 'Listen, mister, I've told you all I know. This morning Andreas told me to watch the Cavalieri and if the lady left'—he glanced at Jenny—'follow her without being seen. I had the car. It was just bad luck you spotted me.'

'We spotted you because you weren't being very clever. Mr Rossi would be interested to know about that, wouldn't he?' suggested Grant.

The man stared at him suddenly. 'You can't do that because you don't know where he is. Nor do I. You can't tell the police because if you did the Englishman would be killed. I can't tell you more, so let me go.'

'To make your report to Andreas?'

'No,' said the man earnestly. 'I'm afraid of

him. I've got money in Corfu. Not much, but enough to get a lift in a caique to Patras. I've got friends there. They'll hide me.'

Grant frowned. The man had spoken as if he was telling the truth. Jenny said urgently, 'Let's leave him, Luke.' They could hear a car approaching on the road behind them, and waited until it had passed.

Grant asked, 'What's beyond these bushes?'

She ran forward to look and came back. 'There's a fairly steep drop with a tangle of scrub at the bottom.'

'Good.' He bent down and pulled the man's shoes off. 'Take these and the contents of his wallet and throw them over the edge. Then get into his car and start the engine.' When she had gone he said, 'You heard that we know all about you, Kellezi. How d'you suppose that is? Because I have friends here among the police, and they're already looking for you in connection with that pimping charge, so you'd better find that caique, and you'd better not talk. Is that clear?' He picked up the little radio and slipped it into his pocket.

The man stared back with fear and hatred in his eyes, but he nodded.

'All right, then. It won't take you long to get your hands free.'

Kellezi said, 'I need the money. You've thrown mine away, but you can give me a few drachmas for the caique.'

'You'll find your own money, though it'll be

77

a rather painful job.' Slipping the knife into his pocket he jumped into the driving seat of the hired car, and called to Jenny to follow him. 'I'll stop soon and we'll talk.'

He drove fast until they were in the outskirts of Corfu, pulled into a side street and turned to the right, so that the cars were out of sight of the road. He stopped and Jenny followed suit. She locked the blue Fiat and slipped into the passenger seat beside Grant. He lit a cigarette and looked at her. 'There's something on your mind, isn't there?'

'That man was lying. At least part of the time.'

'Oh was he? How d'you know?'

'I found this in his wallet.' She took from her pocket a receipt for ninety litres of petrol. 'He must have forgotten he'd kept it for his expenses claim.'

Grant looked, frowning, at the Greek letters. 'What's this mean?'

'The Blue Sea Garage, Gaios, Paxos. Look at the date—last Saturday. That's where Kellezi must have tanked up the yacht, and that's where they took Roger.'

Grant stared at her angrily. 'Then why on earth didn't you tell me? I'd have had the whole story out of him.'

'I—I was afraid you'd carve him up. You looked as if you were quite capable of it.'

'For Christ's sake, Jenny! It wouldn't have come to that. He was talking fast enough

78

already. And I'd swear most of it was true.'

'Yes, but did you notice? After that radio exchange with Andreas—if that's really who he was; I couldn't catch the name—Kellezi was talking much more freely. I'm sure he'd given Andreas a warning, and I was afraid they'd be sending a car to check up—and we've only got that knife between us.'

'But how did he give the warning? He said only what you told him, didn't he?' He started suddenly. 'No all-clear signal, was that it?'

'Exactly. If he'd been trained for radio and wasn't in any trouble, he'd have started with some phrase that meant OK. But he didn't, so Andreas would know he was under duress.'

Grant groaned. 'That's really torn it.' He looked at the girl reproachfully. 'I can't think what's got into you, Jenny.'

'I'm sorry, but I hated that bullying act of yours, and anyway, we're better off as it is.'

'Are we indeed? Just spell that out for me.'

'We can't go to the police—we've discussed that already. But we can go to Paxos without anyone knowing, anyone at all. Andreas will be looking for us on this island, and we can just disappear.' She saw him looking doubtful, and went on quickly, 'I told you Spiro had found out that the KGB had some shack or house on Paxos that they used for training. It's just the sort of place they'd choose to keep someone prisoner. Let's go there and find it.'

'Comb the whole island?'

'It's only six miles long, and the house is on some cliffs, so that narrows it down. Our main job is to release Roger before they can take him away, isn't it? OK, they *may* have removed him to Moscow already, I agree. But there's a chance he's still there, now. We can't afford to wait.'

'How far is Paxos from the southern tip of Corfu?'

'Only ten miles, but it's no good driving down to Cavos; we'd never find a caique to take us across, but here in the port there are plenty.'

Grant thought. 'All right, then. You seem to be the organizer. You tell me what to do.'

'Andreas—if that is the name of Kellezi's control; he may have invented it for all we know—will probably have the number of our car, because Kellezi will have reported it. But he's unlikely to know us by sight, and we have a head start on the wretched barefoot Kellezi. We must leave his car, and ours, some way from the port and find a caique. The regular ferries take two and a half hours to Lakka— that's the northern port on Paxos—but a fast caique might take a bit less; I don't know. We'd better leave the blue car here and drive our car to the square by the Liston arcades, where most of the hired cars are parked. Then I'll find a caique and you pick up some food and drink and meet me on the quay.'

Grant thought it over. 'I think you're right.

80

It's true that if we went to the police, by the time there was any action Roger would probably be dead, since the first thing they'd do is ring the villa and ask Clare to come clean — with someone listening in, no doubt. But it's an awful gamble. All that travelling time wasted, and perhaps Ingram won't even be on the island. Even if he is, what chance have we got with one knife between us? But it's the only lead we've got, and there's just a chance it might pay off. All right, Jenny, I'll accept your plan, but on one condition. When there's any real action, you do as you're told.'

'Aye, aye, sir.'

As they drove into the town the transceiver in Grant's pocket uttered its plaintive call. Jenny turned her head, startled, but he smiled and let the signal continue until after a dozen bleeps it went silent.

Half an hour later they met on the quay, beside the line of moored caiques. Grant was carrying a bag containing crusty bread, sausage and feta cheese, wine, and a large bottle of mineral water. Jenny was talking to a short, stocky man whose faded cotton singlet, once brightly striped, drooped over his hairy chest. Bare feet protruded from patched cotton trousers, but a yachting cap set at a jaunty angle on his grizzled head added a note of authority.

'This is Captain Gremos, Luke. He says we've missed the ferry but he'll take us to

81

Lakka. He's just leaving.' She pointed to a single-masted wooden vessel, its timbers encrusted with salt and with cargo piled on the deck and in the waist. 'I've told the captain we want to get to Lakka quickly and make the most of the light, so he'll use his motor and charge you an extra hundred drachs to cover the fuel. Is that all right?'

A few minutes later they were leaning against some sacks of cement while the port of Corfu and the castle on the headland slipped away across the blue water.

A small boy let out the jib and busied himself with the mainsail, which was bundled along the boom, and as they turned south, with a brisk westerly breeze, the big sail rose and bellied out. The caique heeled over and trembled to the thrust of the wind.

It was a perfect day for sailing, with the sun shining hot on their shoulders. The caique swished through the water, carving out a glassy bow wave with an occasional plunge that sent a refreshing shower of spray over their heads. The island paraded past them in slow motion. First, the town, piled up above the sea, spear-headed by the fortress on its promontory, then the hill of Kanoni, the causeway across the mouth of the Khalikiopoulos lagoon, the big hotels of Perama and the summer palace of the Achilleon on its mountain top. The wooded shore and the hills behind unwound past them like a long scroll. Grant doubted whether the ancient engine added much to their speed, though even a few knots extra were a useful addition. The small boy, his chores completed, had rejoined the captain in the wheelhouse near the stern.

'I'm hungry,' said Jenny suddenly. 'What did you bring?'

He showed her. 'Plenty of wine, too.' Grant was unwrapping a bottle as he spoke, and took it aft to the captain. It was acknowledged with a graceful gesture and some remark in Greek. Jenny was spreading out the food, and he lent her Kellezi's knife.

'You've done us proud,' she said. Under the admiring eyes of the boy, who had come near, attracted by the idea of food, she opened the flick knife and cut hunks from the crisp loaf and laid slices of cheese and sausage between them. 'Gherkins, too,' she said. 'That was a good idea.' She gave a sandwich each to the boy and the captain, who reciprocated with half an onion and some grapes. For some time they ate contentedly.

Grant stretched himself out and lay back with his head on his folded jacket. 'I'm wondering how they got Roger to that house on Paxos, if that's where he is, and I think your theory is a good one. The snatch took place on Saturday morning, we think. If Kellezi was for once telling the truth, Ingram was taken away by boat—that motor-cruiser of Vlasov's—and they probably went straight to Paxos, down the west coast of Corfu and through the straits. But on the way they had to dispose of Spiro's body and make it look as if he'd been chewed up by lobsters. Sorry, Jenny, but you see it is a factor in the time problem. It couldn't be done very quickly. In any case they might have thought it best to wait until nightfall before landing at Gaios. Is it a lonely sort of place?'

'It's the liveliest place on the island. If they took Roger ashore by day it would have to be on a stretcher, if it was at Gaios, in which case we might find someone who'd remember. But perhaps they didn't go there, except to tank up before leaving again for Corfu.'

'Where else could they land?'

Jenny sighed. 'There are only three harbours, Gaios, Lakka and Loggos, which lies between the other two. Lakka is at the northern tip and the nearest place to Corfu. Loggos and Gaios are on the east coast. But there are other places where they could take him ashore, using a dinghy. I suppose any large motor-cruiser would have a collapsible boat aboard. It's no use trying to speculate, Luke; we've just got to hope our luck will hold.'

'I suppose so.' Grant sat up and took a look at her face. 'You've had a hard time, Jenny. Why don't you sleep?' He placed his rolled-up jacket under her head. She curled up beside him and closed her eyes. 'Yes, nanny,' she murmured and within seconds, as it seemed to Grant, she was asleep.

He watched her for a while, then rose and stood near the mast. There was a good deal of traffic in the narrow seas between the Greek mainland and the island. Ferries from Corfu to Igoumenitsa and Patras, cruise ships, fishing boats and yachts of the Islands Sailing Club, all busy on their separate occasions. The coast of Corfu was flatter now, giving way to the long low tongue of Lefkimmi which forms the southern end of the island. Beyond, on the horizon, the coast of Paxos was coming into view.

The caique left the shelter of Corfu for the troubled waters between the islands, where the west wind had piled up the waves. Jenny awoke, and they watched together as the wooded spine of Paxos rose above the water, and the high bows of the caique swayed and plunged. Grant put an arm round the girl's shoulder to steady her, and she looked up at him gratefully. They both knew that in Paxos they might be taking on a little more than they could cope with.

\*       \*       \*

Vlasov sat behind the desk in the living room of Andreas's flat in the old town and looked up as Kellezi was brought into the room. He was a badly frightened man.

Vlasov said coldly, 'You were instructed to follow the targets unobtrusively, and instead you lose them and your car, and maybe your job.'

'They had stopped the car and were sitting talking,' protested Kellezi. 'I didn't see them until it was too late, so I had to drive past. But farther on I parked in some bushes and saw them go by. The man seemed to be having trouble with the car and came back and asked me for help. It seemed quite genuine—but then he jumped me. He must be a professional hit-man; I've never seen anything as fast. Then the girl told me what to say, while this thug leant on the knife.' He saw Vlasov's contemptuous smile and added hastily, 'But I didn't give anything away, and I left out the all-clear signal, *Kyríe*, and I said you headed north, not south. I told him nothing about Paxos.'

'It is a good thing you didn't,' said Vlasov grimly.

'I kept my head, *Kyríe*. I only said what I knew couldn't do any harm. And it wasn't easy, because they knew all about me and said they'd tell the police.'

'What?' Vlasov was startled out of his calm.

'The woman knew of my living in Patras with Elena, and the police charge. She knew I'd been fired by the P & O. She knew everything. But I didn't let it frighten me, *Kyríe*. I gave nothing away.'

'I hope for your sake, Mehmet, that you're telling the truth. If it turns out otherwise you'll be in bad trouble. How did you get away so quickly?'

'The girl had thrown my shoes and money down the ravine. As soon as I'd got the shoes back I didn't wait to find the money but stopped the first car and told the driver I'd been robbed.'

'I see. You say those two English knew that Ingram was alive?'

'Oh yes, *Kyríe*. I told them you'd given me a note for Mrs Ingram warning her what would happen if she talked to the police.'

When the man had been taken away Vlasov sat thinking. Kellezi had been one of the agents chosen by Spiro, who must have told Otfield all about him. That would explain how she'd been able to scare him by showing her knowledge of the pimping charge. And it would have scared him badly, because if the local police heard of it they would have him under prolonged and drastic interrogation before the day was out. So he'd probably told his captors a lot, the lying bastard. There was only one good thing. Kellezi couldn't have said exactly where Ingram had been taken because he didn't know. All he had done was sail the yacht to Gaios and back to Corfu. There was no way Otfield and Grant could know about the Paxos house.

But who was this Lucas Grant? That was the name Andreas had learned from his informant in the hotel. Vlasov groaned. In Athens everything would have been simple.

There might be a dozen Lucas Grants in the electronic memory of the KGB computer in Moscow, but it would have sorted them out within seconds, with potted case histories, and flashed them by crypto-telex to Athens. Vlasov had heard the name somewhere, but could not identify the connection. Luckily, the man didn't seem to be armed, except for Kellezi's flick-knife.

Kellezi. Again, in Athens there would have been no problem. He could have been liquidated unobtrusively or kept under surveillance until his real loyalty could be assessed. But here—Vlasov simply could not afford to jettison one of his few agents. The man would have to be used.

## CHAPTER SIX

The caique was approaching the coast of Paxos, but there was no sign of a port. The low cliffs seemed to be unbroken, even when close enough for Grant to see the spray dashing against the rocks at their base. Then, as the captain steered slightly to port, a narrow entrance appeared and the caique headed for it, still under full sail. As they passed through the neck of the harbour they saw the little quay of Lakka, with houses clustered behind and scattered among the trees of the hillside. On the right, the olives reached right down to two sickles of golden sand shaded by pines. The caique slid across the gleaming lagoon and the sails came down with a rattle as she turned and edged towards a small jetty. The engine went into reverse and they were alongside, watched by a handful of curious children.

Jenny was talking to Captain Gremos as he tied up. 'He says he has a friend in Gaios with a car for hire. He'll go and ring him. There are no cars in Lakka, apparently. It's charming, isn't it?'

It was indeed an idyllic little place, with the calm mirror of the almost land-locked harbour reflecting the silver-grey of the olives. Gremos led them down a narrow passage to a small square. At the further end there was a café, with a few tables set outside under a trellis, where a spreading vine was intertwined with morning glory, its blue trumpets brilliant in the sunshine. They waited until the captain had finished telephoning. He came out of the café beaming. 'My friend's coming at once,' he said. 'You will have no more than a quarter of an hour to wait. You will take coffee with me?'

They thanked him, and sat down at a table under the vine. There were no people around except the very young and the very old, and not many of those. Jenny saw a map of the island pinned to the wall. She detached it and brought it to the table.

They saw that Paxos was shaped like a leaf,

six miles long from north to south and a mile and a half at its widest. The central vein of the leaf was a road joining Lakka and Gaios, with side-roads or tracks connecting it to the small port of Loggos and many small hamlets. Jenny's heart sank when she saw how many there were. 'We'll never explore them all before nightfall,' she wailed.

'We've got three hours of daylight,' said Grant. 'We'll just have to get around as fast as we can.'

The small Toyota, when it arrived, proved to be a shaky little car, but its brakes and engine appeared to function, and they started off. The first seven sideturnings were abortive, and each time they had to turn back to the central road. On its flanks the olive trees, terraced against the slope, shimmered in the hot sunlight. Jenny was silent after a time, and glancing sideways Grant saw her face was strained. 'How can we ever find him, Luke?' she said unhappily. 'I know it's a small island but . . . Let's stop the car and think.'

He drew into the side. The russet-coloured earth beneath the ancient trees was hazed with drifts of tiny mauve-tinted flowers, filling the air with an elusive scent. Jenny got out and sat on the ground, with her arms round her knees, and Grant joined her.

He said, 'We have one solid clue. The house is near some cliffs. There are apparently plenty of those, but the KGB would need to have some sort of access by road, and that narrows the odds. Now, we can ignore every house that's obviously lived in, with washing hanging on a line, and chickens, and pots of flowers—that sort of thing.' Grant bent down and gathered a small bunch of the tiny cyclamen and sniffed at them. 'Rack your brains, girl, and see if you can remember anything else Spiro told you about the hideout where Bulgareos was trained.'

As she sat thinking, at right angles to Grant with her small mouth set and her clearly sculpted face in profile, Grant was reminded of something. He smiled, and behind her back picked some of the tiny bright flowers and gently dropped them on her dark hair. He leaned back to judge the effect.

She was saying, 'I can't remember much, only that it was a lonely place, a small stone house on some cliffs. He was once taken quite close to the edge, and the instructor laughed and said there'd be an easy solution for anyone who gave trouble.' Grant was adding a few more flowers, judiciously, and she turned to stare at him. 'What on earth are you doing?'

'I'm re-creating Winterhalter's portrait of the Empress Elizabeth, with the diamonds in her hair. It's quite a likeness.'

'Well, I hope it ends right there. She wasn't a very lucky lady, was she? Perhaps I'm not, either . . . But wait. What made you think of her?'

'I told you. You look like her. And she used

to come here, I read in Sankey's guide-book. She had a favourite place, high above the sea on the western coast . . .'

'Mousmouli,' she broke in excitedly. 'Luke, mightn't that be it?'

Grant stared at her. 'Jesus! It just might. It's a lonely spot, from the description. But—It's no good, Jenny. Mousmouli's near the southern end of the island. We must be systematic. Let's find some more bloody avenues to explore.'

'No, Luke,' she said emphatically, her face aglow with excitement. 'It's my hunch, and if it's no good we can try the other places on the way back. Come on, let's play my hunch.' She put out a hand and hauled him to his feet.

'OK, then,' said Grant resignedly. They started off again, ignoring the side-roads until they came to the turning that led to the sad Empress's favourite beauty-spot.

The narrow road, almost too rough for motor traffic, ended abruptly near a couple of houses forming the hamlet of Valiantatika. Leading away to the west was a narrow path between high dry-stone walls. Grant turned the car and parked it under the trees.

It was a claustrophobic path, the walls too high for Grant to see over, unless he stood on his toes. For some little way they walked along it in silence, and came to a break in the wall on their right. The gap was closed with planks, criss-crossed and fixed with nails firmly rusted in. Above them was a chevaux-de-frise of thorn branches through which they could glimpse a low stone house, apparently deserted, the peeling shutters hanging askew. They could hear the sound of the waves now.

The path ended abruptly a few feet from the top of the cliff, and the high wall turned to the right to close the tangled garden behind the old house they had seen through the gap.

The view was extraordinary. Several hundred feet down the waves crashed against the black rocks below, atomizing into a soft mist that blurred their jagged outlines. Further out, the sea was a pattern of every cold shade of grey, but as they watched, the setting sun escaped from behind a layer of gold-edged clouds and slid down to touch the flat expanse of cold sea and, like the hand of Midas, change it to gold.

They stood there for a moment in silence. A stray cyclamen blew away in the wind as the girl tossed her hair back from her face. 'It'll be dark in a few minutes, Luke,' she said quietly, 'and we've got nowhere.'

They began to walk back, in single file because of the narrowness of the path, with Grant in front. He came to the gap in the wall, and idly glanced through the thorns at the blank window of the lonely house. As he did so he heard a faint thud, and for a moment saw two hands pressed flat against one of the lower panes. Then they vanished, and again he heard a noise, impossible to define.

He felt for Jenny's hand and pulled her forward, past the gap. 'We'll go on,' he whispered in her ear. 'If anyone's watching they'll see the top of my head retreating, and think we've left. Then we'll double back. Did you see them, too?'

'What?'

'There was someone behind the window. I saw his hands.'

'*Roger's!*' Jenny stopped dead. 'We can get over the wall, Luke. You can lift me ...' He pulled her after him as he walked further down the path.

'And be seen by whoever's guarding him. *Not* a good idea. OK. This is far enough.' He turned and, stooping, they retraced their steps to the place from which they had seen the sunset. Grant crept along the wall at the end of the garden until he found a place where a pine tree, twisted and gnarled by the winter gales, had undermined the wall, which had crumbled into a heap of stones. On the other side, Grant could see that a path had been trodden through the weeds and bushes of the neglected garden. It led to a wooden door, unglazed, in the windowless side of the house.

The silence was unbroken. The wind from the sea was chilly now, and the mist came creeping between the trees. Grant whispered in the girl's ear, 'They won't be able to see me approach from here, so at least I can get to that door. You stay here—'

'No, I'm coming—'

'You're staying here, because if I get collared, which is unlikely, but possible, you can run for the car and bring the police up here.'

'Oh all right, but call me as soon as you can.'

He rose to his feet and ran silently through the bushes to the door and turned the knob. The door did not budge. It had an old and primitive lock, and there was enough space between the door and the jamb for him to insert the strong blade of Kellezi's knife. The wood splintered. He forced back the bolt and opened the door a crack, waited for a reaction, but heard only the muffled boom of the waves below the cliffs. Then came the sound of a strangled cough, followed by a groan.

It seemed to come from a room on the right of the passage, the one with the window where he had seen the spread hands. He ran forward and tried the door. It was locked, but the key was on the outside. For a moment Grant waited, listening, envisaging a possible trap, but there was no sound elsewhere in the little house. He looked round, and saw an open door on the opposite side of the passage. Inside was a bed, with rumpled blankets spread over it, a primus and some cooking things and stores. On a table by the shuttered window stood a small radio transmitter/receiver, exactly like the one Grant had taken from Kellezi. It was a sign he was on the right track, and his heart lifted.

A plastic jerry-can of water stood on a shelf, with tin mugs beside it. He screwed the stopper in tight and picked up the can, hefting it in his hands. It was heavy enough, and would be some sort of protection. It was only then that he turned the key of the locked room and pushed the door wide open.

The light was failing, but there was enough to see a man tied to a chair, which had fallen over. His hands were strapped together at the wrists and a rope had been passed round his waist and secured at the back of the chair. There was something white in his mouth, held in place by a piece of sticking-plaster. He was coughing painfully against the gag.

Grant cut the ropes and let the man pull off the plaster. 'Ingram?' he queried, and the man nodded, still coughing uncontrollably. Grant ran back to the garden door and signalled to Jenny to come.

She came running into the room, took one look at the man sitting on the floor, dazed, his face pale beneath a stubble of beard, and ran towards him . . . Then stopped. 'Roger,' she said softly. It was almost a sob. 'Oh thank God.'

They helped Ingram to sit in the chair, where he sat rubbing his wrists together to restore the circulation. 'He seems to be alone here,' said Grant, trying not to notice the tears in the girl's eyes.

'Not for long,' said Ingram hoarsely. 'Give me some water.' Grant unscrewed the stopper of the jerry-can and held it to the man's mouth. When he had drunk a couple of mouthfuls he pushed the container away. 'There's one guard on at a time. This one's gone to the shop to get cigarettes. He'll be back any minute now.' He seemed to be unaware of Jenny's presence, but looked up at Grant. 'Are you armed? And who are you?'

Grant told him, and added, 'I've got no gun. Has the guard?'

'Oh yes,' came the answer, still in that hoarse, rasping voice. 'He's got a Walther PK, and he's big and a quick mover, as I know to my cost. You'll have to take him by surprise. I'm not likely to be much good on my feet, I'm afraid. They kept me tied up most of the time.' There was a tear in the grimy sweater he was wearing and the sandals on his bare feet, Jenny noticed, were rough and dirty. He went on urgently, 'Is Clare all right?'

'Yes. She's at the villa. Jenny, stay near the window, please, and warn us as soon as you see anyone's head moving along the top of the wall.' He turned to Ingram. 'Now, let's see if you can walk.'

He took him by the arm and made him take steps across the stone floor. Ingram was obviously very stiff in his limbs, but he made some progress.

'Thanks,' he said. 'Listen, Grant. I told you he'd be coming back. What are you . . . ?'

'We'll have a reception committee for him. What worries me is that car of ours. He'll have seen it.'

'If he saw us arrive he'd have turned up here already,' argued Jenny. 'I can't see why we didn't run into him anyway, unless he was in the back of the shop, drinking ouzo with the owner. How did you come to signal to us, Roger? Luke saw your hands pressed to the glass.'

'When I heard your voices I managed to jiggle the chair across to the window. I was going to break the glass with my fists, and if I couldn't attract your attention as you came back at least try to cut the rope. But I lost my balance and couldn't make it.'

'When does the guard change?' asked Grant.

'Ten o'clock tonight. They both have radios, so you must clobber this one before he can warn his pal down in Gaios.'

Jenny jumped back from the window. 'Someone's coming along the path.'

Ingram peered through the dusty panes. 'That's him. Yani, the tall one. He won't be able to see much through this window because it's darker in here than outside, but watch when he reaches the gap in the wall. If he suspects anything's wrong he'll stop there to have a look.'

Tensely, they watched, but the man's head continued to bob along above the wall without pausing at the gap.

'He'll suspect something when he sees that door unlocked,' said Grant suddenly, 'and the marks of the knife on the lock.' He turned swiftly towards the passage. 'I'll leave it wide open. Then he may think we've gone.'

He ran out into the passage and drew the door open, softly, to stop it from squeaking. Then he locked the room Ingram had been in and joined the others in the room opposite, where little light penetrated through the closed shutters. They arranged themselves on either side of the open door, Grant with the jerry-can in his hand.

For a few moments there was complete silence. Then they heard the brushing of legs through the scrub in the garden, and a sudden loud Greek oath. Then silence again. The man was uncertain what to do. But he made up his mind and came forward into the passage.

Grant waited until he heard the man approach the locked door opposite, his hand fumbling for the key, and leapt out into the passage, with the heavy water-container swinging. It struck Yani's back and knocked him forward against the door he had been trying to open. But he had half-turned when he heard the swift movement behind him and the gun in his left hand was already pointing at Grant when it was knocked away, to slide clattering across the stone slabs. Then the man's big hands closed round Grant's throat, and tightened their grip.

Choking, Grant managed to hook his foot behind the other's leg, and they fell, rolling over on the floor, each trying to bring his knee up into the other's crotch. But Ingram had snatched up the automatic and, bending down to seize the man by the hair, pulled his head up and hit it with the barrel of the gun, hard. For the moment, it was enough.

'Thanks,' said Grant, gasping. 'We won't take any chances with this one. Keep him covered.' He hauled on the man's legs and dragged him into the room where Ingram had been kept prisoner. Between them, they bound him to the chair with pieces of the cut rope and lashed it firmly to an iron hook in the wall. As the final knot was tied the man recovered his wits and began to shout and struggle, but Ingram roughly stuck the muzzle of the automatic against the gaping mouth. He subsided.

Grant said, 'We've got nearly four hours before the other guard turns up. The one on duty here doesn't have to make regular reports by radio?'

'No,' said Ingram. 'At least, I never heard them do it.'

'Good. So we leave this one here and tell the Paxos police to come and get him.'

'No,' said Ingram earnestly. 'If we do that

they'll keep us here all night. We've got to get Clare to safety, before they find out that I've escaped, and try and grab her. You said she was at the villa. What's she doing there, for God's sake?'

'She's under duress. I'll tell you later.'

'Under duress? You mean, they're there, with her? My God, if they touch her I'll—But wait. Don't you see, that makes it even more vital to get to the villa, quick, and surprise them. Damn it, we've acquired a gun, and there're two of us.'

'Three,' said Jenny quietly.

'Yes, you of course, Jenny, but you can't do much if there's going to be a scrap. Grant and I can cope, but not if we have to waste time here frigging around with the police. Let's throw this bastard over the cliffs; then he can't tell them anything. It's only what he deserves.' Ingram's voice was rising hysterically.

'Don't be a fool. He stays here. We'll leave a message for the police before we quit the island.'

'All right. I'm sorry, Grant, but I've got a bit worked up. And I don't understand what's happened. How can Clare be—?'

'Let's stop talking in front of this man,' said Grant. 'For all we know he may understand.' He led Jenny and Ingram into the other room. 'Now,' he said, 'this is the main thing. Clare is still at the villa because like that she's under KGB control. As far as you're concerned, she

101

probably thinks you're alive, but the rest of the world thinks you're dead.'

'*Dead!* What are you talking about?'

'First tell me,' said Grant, 'did they kill Spiro?'

'Yes. You see—'

'Later. We can talk about that on the way to Lakka. Clare was made to identify his body as yours, and it was buried, under your name, in the British Cemetery yesterday afternoon. We, and Clare, are the only people who know you're alive, apart from the enemy. Now, I agree with you that the moment the KGB know you're free they'll be attracted by the idea of snatching Clare to make you toe the line, and holding her somewhere secret. But on the other hand they will expect us to have told the police, who will therefore be buzzing around like angry hornets, so Vlasov probably won't dare risk the snatch. What we'll do is to ring the vice-consul and tell him to alert the police and get Clare to safety.'

'I can ring Clare direct, from Paxos, and—'

'That,' pointed out Grant grimly, 'would be the quickest way of warning the KGB that you've escaped. They've certainly got someone at the villa or they'll have tapped the telephone line. No, that's out. We'll have to depend on the V-C, but I think he'll do what's right, and quickly.'

'He's an old waffler,' objected Ingram.

'He's far from it, and you've got to trust

him. Now let's make sure this man Yani can't get away.'

'What we usually do,' said Jenny to Ingram, in a casual voice, 'is throw their money, papers and shoes over a cliff.' She hadn't forgiven him for discounting her value in a tight spot.

Grant laughed at Ingram's baffled expression. 'We had to do just that earlier today. I'll just make sure the knots are tight, and we'd better gag him.'

'I'll do that,' said Ingram. 'It'll be a pleasure.'

'And I think we'll take these blankets.' Grant was stripping them from the bed. 'It could be cold on the boat.'

'What boat?' asked Ingram eagerly. 'Have you got one, then?'

'Only if we can persuade the owner to take us back to Corfu. It's a caique.'

'But that's no good,' said Ingram pettishly. 'We want something fast.'

'What we want and what we get aren't necessarily the same,' said Grant dryly. He was finding this young man a little hard to take.

\*     \*     \*

Five minutes later they left the lonely house and its single unhappy occupant. It was dark now, and the small car was hardly visible under the trees. Jenny helped Ingram, who was still moving stiffly, into the front seat, then hurried

103

round, flipped forward the driver's seat and got in behind.

'We'd better avoid Gaios,' said Grant.

'We certainly had,' agreed Ingram. 'The other guard, Ari, has a room there, and I want to keep out of his way. Is Lakka where you landed?'

'Yes. We'll try to find the skipper or his pal the car owner and see if they can fix us up with a boat. I think, as you say, we must try for something faster than the old caique.'

The road, with its steep gradients and sharp bends, was not so easy now that darkness had fallen and though speed was essential it was equally vital to avoid a pile-up. As the headlights raked the bewildering patterns of stone walling and twisted tree trunks, Ingram told them of the surprise attack by Vlasov on the Mirtiotissa rocks. He and Spiro had been locked up in the blacked-out forward cabin of the motor-cruiser, and somewhere out at sea Spiro had been taken up on deck. There had been sounds of a struggle, and some time afterwards a splash, as something heavy hit the water.

Hours later, in darkness, they had landed in a small cove and Ingram had been taken up a steep path to where a car was waiting. He had been brought to the house at Mousmouli and had remained there, a prisoner, ever since. He had not seen Vlasov again, and there had been no attempt to interrogate him.

Ingram's account tallied quite closely with what Kellezi told them earlier, but he explained, 'I'm just giving you the bare outlines, of course, so that you can understand. I'll fill it in later. What I want to know is more about Clare. Did you see her?'

'We went to the villa this morning. She seemed perfectly well, and not frightened, but there's no doubt that she was under orders from the KGB. She told us how you'd disappeared, and how she'd gone to the police, and then next day 'your' body was found at the southern end of the Mirtiotissa beach, and she'd been called to identify it. Which, she told us, had been made easier by the fact that you had a birthmark which she recognized. Your face had been beyond recognition.'

'And I suppose the birthmark must have been on Spiro. I didn't know he had one.' Ingram laughed shortly. 'They conned her, of course.'

'What do you mean?' said Jenny.

'They certainly wouldn't have set me free after going to so much trouble to arrange my premature demise. You have to hand it to Vlasov—he's bright. But what on earth do you suppose he was going to do with me? And with Clare?'

Grant said, 'It's just a theory, but I think you were going to be declared a defector, and later Clare would have been brought to Russia to join you, like Melinda Maclean.'

'But I wouldn't have played—Oh, I see what you mean. I suppose you think that by the time they'd finished processing me I'd have been just as co-operative as any defector. They'd have gone on and on until they'd wrung the last drop out of me.'

'I'm afraid so.'

The lights of Lakka were twinkling through the darkness. 'We want to keep you out of sight,' said Grant, 'so I'll run the car along the track beyond the quay, and in behind the white building. It's the Nautical Club, I think. Roger and I can wait for you there, Jenny, and you'd better make for Nikko's. If the skipper and his pal are there, ask them to come outside and settle for the car. Here's some money. Then you can make enquiries about a boat. Thank goodness you speak such good Greek.' They were in the outskirts of the little port. 'I'll drop you here.'

Jenny turned up a small lane leading to the square and Grant drove on towards the jetty, crunching softly along the track at the edge of the narrow beach towards the Nautical Club, which shone whitely in the starlight. Lights gleamed here and there in the windows of a house, but the club building was silent, the iron gates closed.

'We'll go right in here under the trees. If the skipper thinks we're acting oddly, we'll have to think of some explanation.' He turned to look at Ingram. 'Are you all right?'

'Just a bit tired, and I could do with a drink. And hungry, too. The meals on Vlasov's boat were pretty basic, but ample compared with my prison cell. But listen, Luke. I want to talk to you.'

'There'll be time on the boat.'

'No, I mean alone.'

Before Grant could reply they heard the crunch of footsteps on the track. It was Jenny, and with her Captain Gremos, who greeted Grant with affectionate warmth. Jenny looked worried. 'There's trouble, Luke. The telephone cable between here and Corfu is out of action. It has been all day, and they don't know when it'll be put right.'

Ingram swore. 'When can he take us to Corfu?' he demanded.

Jenny answered in Greek. 'He can't. Captain Gremos is staying in Lakka tonight—' She saw Ingram about to interrupt and went on quickly, 'But we've had a bit of luck, real luck, because the Captain's nephew Theo has just arrived back with his fast motor-boat. He was going to stay the night with his uncle, but Captain Gremos has persuaded him to take us.'

'When can we leave?' asked Ingram impatiently.

'In about an hour. Theo's got to fill his tank and have some food, and then he'll be ready.'

'What a bloody nuisance!' burst out Ingram. 'Surely he can wait for his grub. Let's tell him to pull his finger out and—'

'I think you'd better be a bit more polite, Roger,' said Jenny shortly, in English. She could see Gremos's manner had lost some of its cordiality. 'Theo's been out all day. It's only the Captain who's been able to fix it. Thank him.'

'Oh all right.' Ingram turned to Gremos and thanked him rather perfunctorily. 'Let's have some food ourselves, if we've got to wait.'

Jenny went into the stone-flagged kitchen of the café. From a large iron pot simmering over the charcoal brazier came a smell that was a savoury blend of shellfish, garlic, oil, herbs and other pleasant things. They sat down around the well-scrubbed table and were served with ouzo and then, with the fish soup, red wine and hunks of dark home-made bread. Ingram's face began to regain some colour, and he lost the querulous look which had so obviously made a bad impression on Grant.

The launch was a fifteen-footer, quite broad, with two bucket seats behind the windscreen and a bench running round the well behind, open to the weather, but adequate for the calm sea they met when they emerged from the landlocked harbour of Lakka and headed north. Theo was a dashing young Greek, very proud of his boat. 'She's called *Lucky*,' he told them, as Jenny took the seat beside him, with Grant and Ingram squatting behind on the floor-boards to avoid the spray.

## CHAPTER SEVEN

Vlasov stared at Andreas incredulously for a moment, then jumped to his feet, pale with fury. *'He's got away?* Am I wholly surrounded by incompetents? Are all of you such morons that you can't even hold a man when he's tied hand and foot? How the hell did he get loose?'

The Greek's eyes were blazing. 'You insult me, *Kyríe,*' he said coldly furious. 'The Englishman and the Otfield woman were there. Spiro must have told her about the training location on Paxos. You said he couldn't have known, but you were wrong, Major. We're not the only ones who make mistakes.'

Vlasov sat down again. This was close to insubordination, but at all costs he must keep Andreas sweet. 'I'm sorry,' he said. 'I did not mean you, Andreas, my friend. But Spiro could not have known. It must have been that cretin Kellezi. I ought to have guessed that he'd keep little back when someone was offering to push a knife into his liver. I'll deal with him later. How did this happen?'

'Ari, the second guard, was due to relieve Yani at ten o'clock. When he reached the house he found Ingram gone and Yani tied and gagged. He went back to Gaios and down to the quay, thinking the English might still be there. But they weren't, and hadn't been seen by anyone. So Ari rang a friend in Lakka, and found out, sure enough, that two men and a woman, English, had just left for Corfu in a launch.'

Vlasov swore viciously. 'What sort of boat?'

'A small one, *Kyrie*, fifteen foot, with a good outboard. They'll make Corfu City in an hour or more.'

'So what did Ari do? Not telephone you, I hope?'

'No, *Kyrie*, he couldn't. The cable had been cut by a trawler.'

'That's something, at least,' said Vlasov, with a sigh of relief. 'But how did Ari let you know, then?'

'He waited—it wasn't long—for the next emergency radio schedule, and gave me the whole story.'

'You can't mean,' protested Vlasov furiously, 'that he made his report in plain language over the air? For God's sake, man, anybody might have picked it up.'

'Yes, *Kyrie*, and he was right. It was an emergency, and he had to get my instructions. There was no time to encode the message—it was far too long. He was right to take the risk of interception. In fact, Ari acted throughout with intelligence and initiative—the qualities for which I recruited him,' added Andreas, rubbing it in.

Vlasov restrained himself. 'But surely the police had been alerted by this time?'

'No, *Kyríe*. Ari sent his wife to the police post with a complaint that his nets had been stolen, but there was no activity there at all. Everything was just as usual, with only the night duty man awake.'

'You mean, for some reason the English didn't tell the police they'd sprung Ingram. Now why, Andreas?'

'Because they knew they'd have been kept on Paxos all night, *Kyríe*, and they wanted to get back to Corfu.'

'Of course!' exclaimed Vlasov. 'That's clever reasoning, Andreas, and I'm sure it's right. Well, if so, that was their mistake. How fast is this boat they're in?'

'It's the *Lucky*, a fifteen foot launch, painted white, with a fair-sized Johnson outboard. It'd take about two hours, or not much more on a night like this, to reach Corfu from Gaios.' He looked at his watch, a present from Vlasov, of which he was proud. 'That's in about forty minutes.' He slapped his hands together. 'Solon's the man. He could use *Hysperia*, that big launch he hires for deep-sea fishing. She's in the old port, but he could take her round to Kanoni and lie in wait for the little boat. And then—if you pay him enough . . .'

'Kanoni? Yes, that's what we'll do. In fact, I'll go with him. It isn't a case of taking prisoners now.' And this time, Vlasov added to himself, there would be no mistake. Solon was a hit-man who would keep his mouth shut; and he knew the seas around the island like his own hand.

When Andreas had gone to find Solon, Vlasov opened a cupboard and reached out a long-barrelled Browning automatic, with a silencer already fitted. He hesitated a moment, then went to a small safe, built into the wall, worked the combination and took out two small objects the size and shape of an egg.

\*     \*     \*

The *Lucky* was making fast time. The wind had dropped, and the surface of the sea was oily dark and smooth, but with the swell that moves perpetually in the straits. The beam from the lighthouse at Cavos, near the southern tip of Corfu, swung rhythmically across the water. The rising moon was half-full, its light sharpening the outlines of the coast and deepening the shadows.

Ingram was now curled up asleep in the well of the boat, his head on a rolled-up blanket. Grant threw another blanket over him. The noise of the outboard made talking difficult, but from time to time Jenny turned in her seat and pointed out to Grant lights marking the places they had passed in the morning. They were nearing Perama, the entrance to the

Khalikiopoulos lagoon opening out ahead of them, and there lay Mouse Island, black and silent.

Ingram awoke. 'We'll soon be in Corfu. I'll go straight to a telephone—' He broke off as a beam of light stabbed through the darkness, blinding them temporarily and giving a helpless sense of exposure. As suddenly as it had come the light was gone, and it was a moment or two before their eyes could adjust to take in the form of a big motor-cruiser that had slid out from behind Mouse Island and was gaining on them steadily. It was a broad, powerful boat, with a flying-bridge above the wheelhouse, and on it they could make out two dark figures. It was *Hysperia*, the boat Solon hired when he took tourists fishing for marlin.

'What's he trying to do?' cried Ingram. 'Ram us?'

Grant shouted to Ingram and Jenny to keep their heads down. If it was Vlasov in that other boat he would be a desperate man, ready to sink the little launch and its passengers without trace. It was only by that means that he could be sure of protecting himself and his operation. Grant crouched in the stern, by the roaring outboard, and steadied Yani's big automatic on the transom. But the movement of the launch made it impossible to sight properly, even if he could have seen the other vessel clearly. And as if the man at the wheel of the *Hysperia* realized this, the searchlight came on again, dazzling Grant's eyes painfully. He closed them for a moment, then opened them, narrowing the lids, and aimed at the blaze of light.

He missed. The searchlight continued its merciless glare, and the big boat astern was coming nearer. They could hear her engines now. Theo was coaxing the last ounce of speed from his launch, which was beginning to plane, bouncing alarmingly on the ruffled waters of Garitsa Bay.

Grant squinted again through narrowed eyes and fired three times in quick succession. He heard a bullet whine past his head and then, above the combined roar of engines, came a double splintering crash, and the light fell dead. The *Hysperia* swerved violently and lost speed.

The searchlight was mounted above the framework of the flying bridge, and one of Grant's shots had missed it, but hit the windscreen below, reducing it to an opaque sheet of crystallised glass. Solon, behind the wheel, was unhurt, but it took him precious seconds to smash a big hole in the screen to see where he was heading. Then he thought that it might be safer down below in the wheelhouse, and jumped down to take his stance behind the duplicate wheel. He began to bring the launch back on course, and Vlasov joined him.

The gap soon narrowed, and Solon took up

114

a position astern and a little inshore of *Lucky*, to make it impossible for Theo to head for the yacht harbour on the near side of the old fort for fear of being rammed.

Suddenly Ingram shouted to Theo in Greek, 'Turn away, *fast*. He's going to throw . . .'

Everything happened very quickly. Grant had hurled himself forward to protect Jenny, pushing her down in her seat, with his arms wrapped round her head. Ingram was sitting staring back, almost petrified, at the dim figure of a man who had emerged from the side-door of the wheelhouse to stand on the narrow strip of deck, holding on with one hand. The other arm was raised to throw, but as he did so his craft struck the stern-wave made by the little motorboat's sudden turn, and his throw fell short by a couple of yards. There was a dull, heavy thud, and a fountain of water was thrown into the air.

'It's Vlasov,' shouted Ingram. 'Give me the gun, Luke. He'll try again.' Grant released Jenny and pushed the Walther into the other man's hands.

But there was no chance of getting in another shot with any hope of success. Theo had turned at right-angles, heading out to sea, and the motor-cruiser had a larger turning circle. Theo was spluttering with rage. 'That was a *grenade*,' he shouted to Jenny. 'I know the noise they make, from fishing. The son of a dog! He'd blow my boat up, would he? Let's see.'

*Hysperia* was almost catching up, still lying inshore of the smaller boat, to stop Theo from making for the port, whose lights had already come into view beyond the dark bulk of the citadel. Then Theo spun his wheel, made a wildly bouncing three-quarters turn to the right, away from *Hysperia*, and cut across her wake. But Vlasov, now at the helm, had foreseen this manoeuvre and turned to port, to head off Theo and force him to alter course again. Both boats were close in under the towering fortifications of the old fort, and *Hysperia* was hard on the launch's tail. This time it was the big Greek, Solon, who issued from the wheelhouse door as they drew closer. He had told Vlasov he was a cricket player, and would not miss with the grenade. It was the last boast Solon was to make.

When the distance was still twenty yards Ingram fired. It was a risky shot in the semi-darkness, and it missed Solon, who was using both hands as he pulled the pin from the grenade. But Ingram's miss had its effect. The bullet struck the jamb of the wheelhouse door and showered both Vlasov and Solon with splinters. Involuntarily, Vlasov's hands jerked at the wheel. Outside, on the spray-wet narrow deck, Solon's stance was none too sure and the boat's sudden lurch, coupled with the angry buzz of the bullet past his head, threw him off-balance. In a panic, he hurled the primed

116

grenade away from the speeding craft, made a grab for support, missed, and went over the side. As his body hit the water, the sea a few yards astern was torn apart by the explosion.

Vlasov put his wheel hard over and began to circle back. But without the searchlight it was difficult to see anything in the churning water, and he had to make up his mind. If he stopped to search for Solon—who might already be dead from the shock wave—*Lucky* would get away, and he, Vlasov, would be in for unending trouble. And though he had not Solon's intimate knowledge of these coastal waters he could handle a motor-boat, none better. He stepped out of the wheelhouse, detached a lifebelt from its hook and threw it into the sea. Then he got back on course, opened the twin throttles wide and let the cruiser surge forward, planing high over the dark water. The gap narrowed rapidly.

Theo was now past the headland, and aiming straight for a line of small craft lying at anchor under the cliffs. Grant thought the man must be planning to slow down and get in amongst them in the shallow water, but there was little time. *Hysperia* was close astern.

Jenny saw Theo cross himself hastily, and the next moment the launch swerved to the left, apparently aiming straight at the base of the fortress wall. While Grant braced himself for what seemed certain to be a crash, he heard Ingram's voice behind him, for once warm with admiration. 'Well done, Theo! Beautifully timed!'

Grant was baffled. It was true that Theo had led the *Hysperia* on until it was too late for the bigger boat to maintain speed and still make the turn, and they heard the note of her engines change. But Grant could see no break in the shore-line ahead . . . Then he saw where they were heading. A silver thread of water opened before them, between a double line of moored boats, and there was a glimmer of star-lit sky above.

It was the channel that served as a moat between the citadel and the Esplanade, crossed at high level by the bridge on which Jenny and Grant had stood the previous evening, and bordered on the landward side by a narrow strip giving access to the boats tied up along the waterway. And this was what *Lucky* was now entering at speed, setting the tethered craft rocking and clashing together as she passed between them. With the towering rock walls closing in on them Theo throttled back, though to his passengers the boat still seemed to be travelling dangerously fast. But how, thought Grant, could Theo be sure the other boat would not follow? Perhaps the water was too shallow, or . . .

Ingram shouted, 'My God, he's after us!'

Incredulously, Theo twisted his head round to see the tall outline of the motor-cruiser against the lighter patch of sky. As he turned quickly back to peer into the gloom ahead he was laughing maliciously. *'He can't know*, then. He'll get a lesson he won't forget, and serve him right!'

They were speeding under the high bridge when Jenny glimpsed something ahead, low over the water, and shouted to the two men behind her, 'Keep your heads *down*, for heaven's sake!'

Then it loomed in front of them, a footbridge, heavy planks resting on iron girders, and only four feet above the water. In fact, there was headroom enough for those in *Lucky*, which sped through untouched. But for Vlasov, and *Hysperia*, there was no escape from disaster. He was only twenty yards away when he first saw the obstacle, and though he reversed the screws, the momentum of the big boat was far too great, and she was still moving at five knots when she hit the nearer of the two girders supporting the footbridge with a crash that reverberated clamorously between the narrow walls of the moat. The bows had scraped under the bridge, but her rail was smashed flat and the hatch-cover of the forward cabin crumpled like matchwood, bringing the heavy craft to a shuddering, grinding halt with the staved-in front of the wheelhouse jammed against the girder.

*Hysperia* was a write-off—and Vlasov, too, was Theo's hope. The pursuit was over, but he had every reason to get away fast. 'I'll drop you at the Yacht Club moorings over there,' he said hurriedly to Jenny. They were emerging from the channel now, and hugging the sea-wall of the Esplanade to reduce the danger of being seen.

As the boat drew in to the jetty all three jumped out. They wrung Theo's hand, and Grant pushed a roll of notes into it. 'Thanks, Theo,' he said hastily. 'Is that enough?'

But Theo stuffed the money, uncounted, into his pocket. 'You have never met me, mister. You understand?' Grant nodded. The outboard sprang into life and soon, relieved of her load, *Lucky* was planing out into the bay, the sound of her engine dying away as she vanished into the night. She had lived up to her name.

They reached the Esplanade at the top of the steps breathless and still shaken. 'We'd better take it easy now,' said Grant. 'No-one will notice us if we stroll along casually like any other tourists.'

'Tourists!' Jenny's heart was thumping, but she smiled. 'Roger's the odd one out. He looks like a hippie with that beard, even if,' she added unkindly, 'he is a bit old for the part.'

They leaned on the balustrade overlooking the sea. Grant said, 'I haven't been so frightened for a long, long time.'

'Because you weren't in charge,' observed Jenny.

'Yes, I suppose it was partly that. But I don't

want to repeat the experience.'

Lights were flashing now from the direction of the fortress bridge, and they could faintly hear shouted orders. A police car, its roof-lamp twirling, came scorching along the coast road, and they could hear it stop at the sentry-post by the bridge. A siren wailed from another direction. But for the three of them, after the perils of that sea-chase, everything seemed unreal. They were no longer part of the action—just spectators.

'Where did you leave your car, Luke?'

'In the Liston park. But why? Our first job is to contact the police.'

'There's no time for that now, man.' Ingram's voice rose. 'Masov must have been warned of my escape soon after we left Paxos, since Ari surely had radio communication with Corfu. God knows what they've got up to in those two hours. Even if Vlasov's dead, Clare may still be in danger. If we go to the Astinomion Polion—police headquarters—right away, by the time they've got a responsible officer awake and on the job it'll take hours. With the car I can get to the villa in twenty minutes. The only thing is—I'd be very grateful for your help. You see, Clare may be guarded, and they'll have to be taken by surprise. I'd do it alone, but with you I'd at least stand a chance.'

'That's very handsome of you, Roger,' said Jenny drily. 'And I'm coming with you, too.

You're not going to leave me out of the action.'

'I'm afraid I am,' said Ingram. 'You'll skip across to the Cavalieri and get your head down. Keep your door locked and don't open it to anyone. We'll see you in the morning.'

'I'm not going to be left behind,' asserted Jenny stubbornly.

'I'm sorry, Jenny, but that was an order. You're dead beat, and this is a man's job.'

In the circumstances, it was an unwise remark. Jenny flared up. 'You're not my boss now,' she said in a sullen voice.

'Maybe not, but I'm senior, so no nonsense, please. just make for the Cavalieri. We'll watch you cross the road, so you'll be quite safe.'

Too angry to reply, Jenny walked away without a backward glance.

Grant had listened to this exchange without intervening. Now he said, 'Did you have to be so bloody patronizing, Roger? After all, the girl is an officer.'

'That doesn't mean she has to be under our feet all the time,' said Ingram ungraciously.

The chill of the October night had driven the Corfiots indoors. and they met no one as they walked down the Kapodistriou towards the Liston. The cafés were closed and shuttered, the chairs piled up on the tables, but there were still a number of cars in the park across the road. The small Fiat was under the trees where Grant had left it.

A few moments later they were on the corniche road, and approaching the old port. Ingram gave directions, and the car picked up speed.

Grant said, 'You were a little hard on Jenny. You owe her a lot, you know. But I agree it was right to make her take some rest.'

'That wasn't the only reason,' said Ingram.

Grant half-turned. 'What d'you mean?'

'I mean,' said Ingram slowly, 'that Spiro suspected Jenny of double-crossing.'

It was all Grant could do to keep his eyes on the road. 'What absolute balls! You didn't believe him, did you?'

'I'm just telling you what he said. He was always hopelessly inquisitive, and one day he saw Jenny in a shabby street in Athens, and followed her. She was obviously nervous, and looked over her shoulder now and then as if afraid of being followed. But Spiro had been well trained—by me,' added Ingram wryly— 'and he kept out of sight while he shadowed her. She disappeared into the entrance of an old house—he gave me the address—and Spiro slunk into a doorway and waited. She didn't come out. Then a car drove up and Vlasov got out and went into the same house.' Grant was silent. Ingram went on defensively, 'That's what he *said*. I don't say I believe what he deduced from it.'

'I'm glad to hear that,' said Grant coldly, 'because you'd be a bloody fool if you did. For heaven's sake, man, there are a dozen explanations. Spiro said he was keeping out of sight, which means some distance away, so he may have been mistaken. Lots of girls in with-it shirts and slacks could look like Jenny from behind—if their shape was as good. Or he could have been mistaken about Vlasov. And there's another reason why Spiro should say what he did. He knew he had no right to go over the head of his new case officer and contact you direct, so he had to think up some convincing excuse.'

'All right, all right. Don't get so worked up about it. I just have to bear the suspicion in mind. After all, how was it that Vlasov knew Spiro was coming to see me, and exactly where? Why was his yacht so near at hand, all ready for the snatch?'

'If Kellezi was telling the truth, all Vlasov knew was that Spiro was going to Corfu, and he probably only learned that at the last moment, because otherwise he'd never have let him leave the mainland. Arrived in Corfu, Kellezi found Spiro was at the Calypso and discovered that Spiro tried twice during Friday to ring someone with a Paleocastritsa number but in the end got through and made an appointment for Saturday. He told his control and the following day, when he pursued Spiro to Paleocastritsa, Vlasov was already there, with his yacht, in the bay. Now if he'd had any warning from Jenny—it's too ridiculous, but let's say he had—he could have picked up Spiro in Corfu, or Paleocastritsa, or anywhere rather than let him actually meet you and hand over his information. Don't tell me he couldn't have done that far more conveniently than run all the risks he ran. That sea-snatch was a last-minute, desperate measure.'

'You sound convincing, but you know as well as I do, Luke, that in our trade any information that seems to compromise a colleague must be followed up ... We're getting near now. You seem to have got the route all right, but don't overshoot the turning in the dark. It's easy to miss.'

'Thanks, but it's too risky to drive near the villa. We'd better leave the car on the road and walk the rest.' A little later he pulled the Fiat onto the verge. The two men closed the doors quietly and Grant locked the car. Then they stood listening for half a minute, but there was no sound of a car following; only the cry of a small night animal and the rustle of dead leaves broke the silence.

A hundred yards further along the road they found the turning to Mirtiotissa. The criss-cross pattern of leaf shadow blurred its outline. 'How right you were,' said Grant in a low voice. 'I could have driven straight past it.' There was danger ahead—for someone, anyway, and Grant knew that he and Ingram must pull together; somehow friction must be avoided.

The moon was high now and where the

track was open to the sky their shadows fell blackly on the dust which was helping to muffle their footsteps. Grant was still struggling with his anger at Ingram's suspicion of Jenny, but he gave him grudging approval as a tracker. All the stiffness in his limbs must have disappeared. The man moved like a cat, without displacing a stone.

They reached the spot where the path led up to the villa, and into the shadow of the trees that branched over it. They went slowly, pausing now and then to listen. The absence of all human sounds was almost unnerving, when they felt that someone must be there.

Ahead, the white walls of the villa glimmered through the tangled vines on the terrace; the shutters were closed, and no light filtered through the slanted bars. They came to the end of the path, and at a sign from Grant separated, patrolling round the house in opposite directions. At the rear they met, and each shook his head. In the moonlight Grant could see that Ingram's face was taut with anxiety. They went on to the terrace and Grant pointed to the door.

Ingram tried the latch. It yielded, and he pushed open the door. Grant followed, his gun in his hand, knowing that if the KGB men were there he and Ingram were hopelessly exposed. But there was no one. Ingram ran distractedly from room to room, calling his wife's name, without response. Drawers were open, clothes strewn on the bed. There were all the signs that someone had made a hasty pack of a few essentials and left.

On the table in the living-room was a transceiver, like the one Grant had taken from Kellezi. It bore a notice, DO NOT ALTER THE FREQUENCY, and beside it was a note, written in English, in block capitals: GO BACK TO THE HOTEL. SPEAK TO NO ONE OR YOUR WIFE WILL SUFFER. WE WILL CONTACT YOU BY RADIO AT NINE TOMORROW MORNING.

Grant picked up the telephone. 'Don't call the police!' cried Ingram, trying to snatch the receiver away.

'I can't,' said Grant slowly. 'The line's cut.' He shook his head. 'We've made a bad mistake, Roger, by jumping to conclusions. If Vlasov himself isn't alive and active, someone else is, and evidently not afraid that we've already gone to the police.'

'I don't understand,' muttered Ingram, sitting on the sofa with his head in his hands. 'If they were here, why didn't they ambush *us*, and knock us off? Why bring Clare into it? She knows nothing.'

'Because,' said Grant, 'they want to get us both in their own time. And if possible, alive. But first they had to shut our mouths. And they must know Jenny's still around. She's just as important. They know I'm armed, so they grabbed Clare as a hostage. If we're to get out of this jam alive, Roger, we've got to keep cool and box very, very clever.'

## CHAPTER EIGHT

Just before *Hysperia* crashed Vlasov had thrown himself down on the deck of the wheelhouse, and though badly shaken was unhurt. The engines were still in reverse, and he staggered to his feet and opened the throttles wide, frantically hoping that the bows would disengage. But they were securely wedged under the bridge. He pushed open the wheelhouse doors and heard shouting high above his head and the sound of heavy military boots running onto the high bridge. Someone was calling for a torch. Vlasov knew he had to get under cover fast.

He stumbled over the wreckage on the foredeck, climbed on to the footbridge and ran back along the bank of the canal ... The farther he could get away from the scene the better and, sure enough, when he turned his head he could see a strong beam of light stabbing downwards at the wrecked motor-cruiser. Vlasov flung himself down and waited until the light was switched off and he could hear men coming down the steps from the citadel high above his head. Then he rose to his feet and ran towards the end of the canal, where he could see some sheds. One was open, and he dived into it and hid, listening to his thumping heart-beats and trying to think out what to do.

With Ingram free, and back on Corfu with his rescuers, there was nothing to stop the English from informing the police and getting Mrs Ingram to a place of safety. On the other hand, wouldn't Ingram be likely to go and find his wife first, without any delay? He would know what time could be lost in contacting the Astinomion Polion. It was a chance worth taking.

Vlasov had no idea how much Spiro had communicated to Ingram before they were captured—it could not have been much—but in any case Spiro had no knowledge of Vlasov's centre of operations, the villa on the coast. That was one safe haven; another was Andreas's apartment in the Kambielo.

He still held one vital card, and a plan slowly formed in Vlasov's mind that could turn rout into victory. But for the moment he must be patient. He settled down to watch.

The men around the boat were chattering and laughing, and seemed more concerned with the novel plight of the cruiser than with the problem of what had been the fate of her helmsman. Vlasov left his shed on all-fours and slowly made his way to the edge of the canal, where he let himself into the water. It was very cold and made him gasp, but he swam silently out into the bay and turned left towards the rusty iron staircase which he had seen from his hiding place. It ran from sea-level up the face of the cliff to the gardens of the Palace of St Michael. He reached the foot of the stair, hauled himself out and climbing over a locked gate got his feet on the iron steps and made his way upwards, concealed from any inquisitive eyes by the bushes that grew closely around the stair. He came out into the silence of the garden, and breathed a sigh of profound relief. He was only three hundred yards from Andreas's apartment.

## CHAPTER NINE

As they drove back towards Corfu town, Grant made up his mind. He must convince Ingram that any suspicion of Jenny was groundless. 'When we were getting away from Paxos,' he said, 'Jenny told you we only suspected something was wrong when we saw Kellezi's car following us.'

'Yes, but then you said later that Jenny's womanly instinct had already made her suspect Clare was fabricating the story. I thought that pretty thin; you were just giving Jenny credit, weren't you?'

'No. Far from it. I couldn't give the real reason in front of Clare, and I wasn't going to tell you either. Because it's Jenny's secret, as well as yours.'

Ingram stopped. 'What exactly d'you mean?' he asked coldly.

'Clare had to identify Spiro's body, but they wouldn't show her the face, because it was unrecognizable anyway. They pointed to a birthmark on the groin. Poor Clare had to say it was proof the body was yours . . . But Jenny knew it was proof that it wasn't.' Grant had no wish to see the expression of Ingram's face. He said roughly, 'Come on, Roger. We've no time to hang about.'

Ingram caught him up. He said between his teeth, 'So little forsaken Jenny—I'm sure she told you the whole story—had to explain that she and I had been lovers.'

'Don't be a bastard, Roger. It's literally true what you just said, she *had* to, to convince me that you might still be alive. It wasn't easy for her, but it was all the proof I needed.'

'I'm sorry. I shouldn't have said that, but— anyway, I agree that it seems to put Jenny in the clear.'

'There was never the slightest doubt of it . . . Now, what exactly is in this report we're looking for? Or are you going to apply the rule of need-to-know?'

'Of course not, Luke, as far as you're concerned. In fact, it's better I tell someone, in case I'm clobbered before I can get back to Head Office with the report. About a fortnight ago Vlasov told Spiro he wanted his help in contacting the smugglers who run goods from Greece into Albania for the black market. You know where Epirus is?'

'It's the long tongue of Greek mainland that runs along the coast below the Albanian mountains. It's what you see from Corfu.'

'Exactly. And that's where the smugglers' bases are. Many of them are related to Greeks in the Albanian hinterland, who have redentist aspirations. Vlasov said he planned to use the smuggling routes as an alternative way of getting men out of Albania, for training, and getting men and arms in. The smugglers could be told they'd be helping a pan-Hellenic movement in Albania. In fact, the Russians want to foment a revolt among the Greek-speaking Orthodox inhabitants of the south, and then escalate it to a national revolution against the present regime in Tirana. So-called mercenaries and weapons-containers would be flown in to help, and the Moscow line would be imposed gradually through a national liberation front. I imagine the whole operation is half of a pincer movement, with a similar revolt being caused in the Muslim parts of the country. After all, seventy per cent of the people are believers in Islam, and they're being persecuted and ripe for rebellion. But this is just what I think, not what Vlasov said.'

'You can't mean that Vlasov *told* Spiro all this?'

'Well, he did, as far as I could make out. He

had to get his collaboration, and he knew Spiro was intelligent enough not to believe the Russians were just out to help the Greek-speakers out of sheer benevolence. But I can't be sure how much Spiro got from Vlasov and how much from other sources. But to go on. Vlasov told Spiro that plenty of money would be forthcoming, and he still wanted him to go on spotting tough young men with Albanian relations, and they had to be good swimmers and Orthodox believers, not Catholics.'

'Jenny told me Spiro's job was spotting young men, but she didn't tell me they had to be swimmers. That's interesting.'

'Yes. It was the first time Vlasov had mentioned it. He'd probably found that his recruiters in Greece were being put in touch with too many youngsters who either couldn't swim or weren't prepared to act as sea-borne infiltration agents, because that's what he went on to explain. He said Spiro could go a bit further when he thought he'd found a likely man, and tell them that if they proved suitable during training they might be set ashore on the Albanian coast, to look up their relatives and find out what the Greek minority thought of the Hoxha regime. Then make their way back over the mountains. That was where the smuggling routes would come in. They would be paid very generously—and Spiro would get a handsome bonus for everyone who made the grade. He could say the whole thing was a fact-finding exercise, but of course that was just the cover story.'

'And if one of them blabbed to the police, Spiro would carry the can?'

'Exactly. Vlasov was just shedding part of the risk. When Spiro pressed him, saying he had to have more to go on, Vlasov said the men would be dropped by boat near the Albanian coast, so the risk of interception was slight. The coast is very little inhabited, so the plan isn't quite as suicidal as it sounds, and it's true that there are lots of tough young Greeks without work who would be willing to risk their lives for a lot of money.'

'Hm,' said Grant. 'And Spiro had agreed?'

'He had, but not just for the bonus. He asked for, and got, a much bigger salary because of the extra risk he'd be running in even approaching men with that sort of proposition. He didn't tell me how much, but of course he asked me to get him a similar rise from SIS.' Ingram laughed. 'Poor Spiro! He never passed up a chance of making a fast buck.'

## CHAPTER TEN

It was still only half-past two when they reached the hotel. The reception clerk looked at Ingram's ill-shaven face curiously. Grant said, 'My friend had a motor accident and his papers got lost. We'll be seeing the vice-consul later about a temporary passport. In the meantime he'll just sign the register, OK?'

'Certainly, sir.' He looked down at Ingram's scrawled, invented signature. 'Your key, Mr Ridley. Number twenty-four. Mr Grant, there's a letter for you. It was brought in by a little boy half an hour ago.'

They took the lift to the second floor. As they passed a door with a DO NOT DISTURB notice hanging on the handle Grant pointed. 'Jenny's room. We'd better see if she's awake.'

At his first knock there was no reply, and Grant's heart sank. He knocked louder, and after a pause they heard Jenny's voice. 'Who is it?'

'Luke. Let us in.'

As she opened the door she was still dabbing at her face with the corner of the bath towel which was wrapped round her like a sarong. She shook her hair back. There was something fresh and wholesome about Jenny, thought Grant—something he had missed when she was not there. But her eyes were on Ingram's set face. She said, 'Where's Clare?'

'They've got her,' said Ingram curtly, turning away.

Grant explained. 'When we got to the villa they'd gone off with Clare, leaving a note. They'll get in touch with us here by radio.' He pulled the little transceiver from his pocket.

135

'With this.'

'Oh Luke,' said Jenny unhappily, looking at Ingram, whose face was still turned away. 'We're back at Square One.'

'I'm afraid so.'

Ingram said suddenly, 'That letter, Luke. What's in it?'

Grant opened the envelope and read the sheet of paper inside it, frowning. He said, 'It's headed, "For Ingram", in block capitals, and then there's a note in longhand, which starts 'Dear Tiger'. Is that you?'

'It's a name she calls me sometimes,' said Ingram, flushing. 'Give it to me.' He read it through slowly, hesitated for a moment, then handed it to Grant.

It ran, 'Dear Tiger, I'm all right so far, darling, but I'm scared. Please *do what they say and don't try anything*. Don't tell the police or the V-C. If you do *they'll know*. Wait for their call. I want you back, so. much. Clare.' The underlining was heavy, and expressive.

Grant handed the note to Jenny who read it, her face colouring slightly and passed it back to Ingram. She said quietly, 'What do we do now?'

'We go to bed,' said Grant. 'There's nothing we can do till the morning and we all need sleep. Off you go.'

\*     \*     \*

They had finished breakfast and were back in Grant's room. Jenny was scanning the two Corfiot newspapers they had bought from the hall-porter while Ingram, who had obviously slept little, was lying on Grant's bed, his eyes closed.

Jenny exclaimed, 'Here's something. It's in the Stop Press column and not printed, just put in with a rubber stamp.' She translated rapidly for Grant's benefit. 'It says the powerful motor-launch *Hysperia*, belonging to Doctor Stavros Papadopoulos, the well known Corfu pediatrician, was engaged in a collision last night with the small footbridge that crosses the moat between the Old Fort and the Esplanade. The circumstances of the accident are mysterious, and the Astinomion Polion are making enquiries.'

'When can we hear the local news on the radio?' asked Grant.

Jenny riffled through the pages of the newspaper. 'There's a bulletin at nine o'clock.' She looked at her watch. 'In ten minutes.'

'Good. That might give us a line.' Grant looked at Jenny quizzically. 'You couldn't, just for once, forget your officer status and take down the bulletin in English, could you?'

She smiled at him. 'Just for once. I'll go and get a writing pad.'

When she had gone Ingram said irritably, 'I don't see what good it can do. You don't think Vlasov's left his signature over everything, do

137

you?'

'No. But any line at all is worth something to us at this stage.'

The mention of the accident came at the end of the main news, and when it was over Jenny read out her English transcript.

'Mystery surrounds two strange, perhaps interconnected happenings that took place last night in the dark waters surrounding the base of the Old Fort. The *Hysperia* is a fast motor-launch, fitted for deep-sea fishing and owned by Doctor Stavros Papadopoulos, the well-known Corfu pediatrician, who is a devotee of the sport. He occasionally allows Solon Gastouri, an experienced fisherman, to hire the launch for the purpose of taking tourists on fishing trips, and this is what the doctor did last night. Gastouri rang him late in the evening, and said he had a rich client who wanted to take advantage of the calm weather and fish for tunny in the Straits during the hours of darkness. The doctor agreed, at a price, and Gastouri came for the keys of the launch and paid the appropriate fee on behalf of his client, whom he did not name.

'At about half-past twelve the launch was driven at speed into the narrow channel between the Old Fort and the Esplanade and struck the footbridge which connects the two sides of the channel. Whoever was sailing the launch evidently did not know of the existence of the little bridge, which is far too low to allow a craft of the size of *Hysperia*, with a flying-bridge as well as a tall wheelhouse, to pass under.

*'But no one knows who the helmsman was.* No one was found on the scene of the crash when the military guard on the high bridge appeared, and there seemed no way in which anyone could have escaped. Doctor Papadopoulos cannot believe that Gastouri, an extremely experienced sailor, could have been responsible—unless he was drunk at the time. All attempts to find Solon Gastouri have so far failed, and a sinister note is struck by the fact that east of the Old Fort, some way from the land, a lifebelt was picked up in the sea early this morning. It bore the legend— "HYSERIA"'!'

They looked at each other in silence when she had finished speaking. Then Grant said, 'Well, we've got a line, even if it's pretty tenuous. It was Solon Gastouri who went over the side, he must have caught the shock wave when the grenade exploded, and we know he didn't connect with the lifebelt Vlasov threw him, and that he's missing. I think he must be dead, and it won't be long before his body floats up and is found. Now if he can hire a boat that size for his foreign clients he might well have a telephone. Let's have a look.'

Jenny was just picking up the telephone directory from the bedside table when there was a bleep-bleep noise from the little radio that stood beside it. Ingram crossed to the bed in two strides and picked up the set. The other two came near enough to hear the reedy voice at the transmitting end. 'Is that Ingram? Over.' The voice was speaking English, fluently, with a slight Slav accent.

Roger switched to transmit. 'Yes, Vlasov.' He moved the switch.

'Owing to circumstances I could not control Katastari had the opportunity of speaking to you for some minutes before we pulled in. I don't know how much he told you, nor whether you have already imparted it to Miss Otfield and her muscle-man Grant. It doesn't matter. I must assume that all three of you know too much for the safety of my plans, which, solely as a result of your interference, will have to be changed radically. My attempt to liquidate you, all three of you, last night failed, and I admit I am not in a position to try this neat solution again.

'But on the other hand, I have your beautiful wife—Be quiet, Ingram. Listen. I need twenty-four hours. If during that time any one of you takes action to alert the local authorities—I'm aware that you haven't done so yet—I shall quickly know, and your wife will suffer. I am a humane man, Ingram, but if you double-cross me I assure you that when you see your wife again you will not recognize her.' The hand holding the set was trembling, but Ingram kept it close to his ear. 'During these twenty-four hours you will not inform any authority that you are alive. You will all three act naturally, as tourists enjoying the sights of this historic city. Of course you will be followed, but I shan't interfere as long as you do exactly what I say, and persuade the others to do the same. That may not be easy, but you must persuade them to follow your example. If all goes well, this time tomorrow your wife will be returned to you, in perfect condition. Do you understand? Over.'

Ingram moved the switch and said in a low voice, 'Listen, Vlasov. I must have proof that my wife is alive and well. Otherwise I refuse your terms.'

'No problem. Go to the window, *now*, and look down. You will see her.'

Clutching the receiver Ingram strode to the window, jerking aside the net curtains. Traffic was streaming along the wide road that separated the hotel from the gardens of the Esplanade. A blue Toyota was parked beside the kerb on the far side, and beside it stood Clare. She was looking up at the hotel windows, and made a faint gesture of recognition. As she did so a sallow-faced man in a dark shirt, white tie and white-rimmed sunglasses reached out an arm and pulled her firmly into the car, which took off fast.

The transceiver bleeped impatiently. Vlasov's voice came on again. 'There, you see. We have good care of her. Remember my

141

instructions, or she may not be so lucky.'

Ingram was sitting on the edge of the bed, staring at Jenny. 'Did you telephone anybody while we were away?' he demanded.

'Telephone? Of course not. We'd agreed not to ring the V-C until you'd rescued Clare. Why on earth d'you ask?'

'I don't understand how Vlasov knew we were on our way to the villa. Even if he'd got away from his boat very fast, which is unlikely, how could he have reached the villa before we did, with time to make Clare pack some clothes and go with him? It doesn't make sense, unless—'

'Unless *what*?' asked Jenny angrily. 'What d'you think I had to do with it? D'you think I warned Vlasov? Is *that* what you're suggesting?' Her eyes were flashing dangerously.

'I don't say—' began Ingram. 'I don't suggest you deliberately—'

'Roger,' said Grant, very firmly, 'you'd better not say anything more. I'll tell you how Clare was snatched. You don't suppose they had *no one* in your villa with her, do you? Where are your wits, man? As soon as Vlasov got to a telephone he rang the villa and gave orders to his chap there to get Clare away before we arrived.'

Ingram was silent. After a moment he got up. 'I'm sorry, Jenny. Luke's right. That's what must have happened. I'm afraid I'm just about all-in, so if you don't mind, Luke, I'll go to my room for half an hour and kip down.' He walked to the door and went out.

'Did you hear him?' cried Jenny furiously. 'How could he? What does he think I am? He's still not convinced I didn't double-cross you both.' She was on the verge of tears.

Grant reached out and took her in his arms. 'He's just had too much,' he said. 'You mustn't blame him for thinking such arrant nonsense.'

She threw her arms around his neck and kissed him, and this time it was no mere peck on the cheek. 'Oh thank God for you,' she muttered. 'You've got to help us, Luke.'

'Of course.' He returned her kiss, taking his time, until she drew away, looking at him rather uncertainly. 'Now listen. First, security.'

'Yes, Luke,' she said submissively. 'But what, exactly?'

'We'll stick to this room for discussions. You've been trained. We'll both check that there's no mike. It's unlikely, but Vlasov obviously has someone in this hotel, if only to know that we didn't telephone to the police, so it's worth having a check.' He pulled out his penknife and opened a screw-driver blade. 'Start with the handset.'

She took off the bottom plate of the telephone receiver and keeping the receiver in its place examined the circuits underneath. 'It's OK. There's no neon.'

Grant carefully checked the light bulbs and

143

the standing lamp. Then they went round the walls. 'It's unlikely to be anything sophisticated,' he said. 'More likely a little radio mike they could put into the room at a moment's notice.' He pulled out the bed and looked behind the radiators, but found nothing. Jenny went over the walls, shifting pictures and curtains, and examined the built-in-wardrobe.

They were still working when the door opened and Ingram appeared. He stood for a moment in the doorway, watching them.

Jenny was near to tears as she looked at his downcast face. She moved her hand, as if to touch him—then drew it back. 'I do know what you're feeling, Roger,' she said slowly, 'but you mustn't just give in. Luke's going to help us to find Clare.'

'But that's impossible. There's nothing we can do. If we leave here we'll be followed. Vlasov said so.' He turned to Grant for support.

'Yes. He said quite a lot, and some of it's worth thinking about. Let's all sit down ... That's better.' He looked at them, Jenny sitting in the large armchair, Ingram perched on the edge of the bed, both of them tense. The very intimacy, he realized, that had bound them together a year ago was going to make it all the more difficult to induce them to collaborate now. There were too many flash-points.

'At the moment,' said Grant, 'we've got nothing else to do, so let's think. Let's put ourselves in Vlasov's place, for a start, and we see at once why he made that personal attempt to rub us all out last night. It was the act of a desperate man, wasn't it? Think of the risks he ran. We had a gun, he knew that, and there was the chance that another craft could have come by at any time. So why did he do it? Because he faced not only the failure of his mission, but humiliation, ridicule and disciplinary action. Add it up, and you'll see what I mean. He was running an informant Spiro, who turns out to be a British double agent. He fails to stop the man from contacting you, Roger, and giving away precious secrets. OK, he kills Spiro and holds you prisoner—but then lets you escape and pass on Spiro's information to Jenny and me. And finally, when he has a good chance of liquidating all three of us, he muffs it, and lets a Corfu boatman lead him into a trap from which he escapes with a launch smashed and half the island police looking for him. You see what I'm getting at? He's made such a mess of everything that if he can't produce a trump card now his colleagues in Dzerzhinsky Square will be laughing their heads off when they hear the news.'

'He's got a trump card,' said Ingram. 'Clare.'

'Yes, for putting pressure on us, but that's

145

not enough. The vice-consul was going to take care of Clare today, when she told him she'd be coming to Corfu to catch the London plane. By now he'll be wondering what's happened, so he'll ring the villa. No answer. So he'll think she's on her way. But she doesn't turn up, he gets worried, checks with the airport and rings the police. Then there's your missing passport, Roger. If you can't produce it the tourist police will get curious. Once they suspect you're holding out on them they'll start checking your movements, and then they'll really get interested. You signed in as Ridley. But who is this Ridley?

'Vlasov must also be scared of police enquiries into the boat crash, and the death of Solon, if and when his body's discovered. The media are on to a mystery, and they'll expect action by the police. And people will come up with stories. Maybe someone saw Vlasov board that launch last night, or Solon talked about his rich client, or one of Vlasov's minor agents gets scared and begins to talk. By this time tomorrow there'll be a whole bunch of loose ends, and some of them will tie up. Vlasov knows this, and also that the moment the local police realise there's something fishy going on, Special Branch men will be flying in from Athens, and starting to comb the island. And it's not very large anyway. Just a whiff of a Soviet plot to use a Corfu base for operations against Albania, and the Greeks will pull out all the stops.'

'I agree to all that,' said Ingram impatiently. 'So Vlasov has to act fast. In fact that's what he told me—he needed twenty-four hours to wind up his operation.'

Jenny said, 'No, what he said was that his plans would have to be radically changed, and he'd want twenty-four hours to do it in.'

'That's what he said,' agreed Grant, 'but he meant us to conclude, as Roger did, that he'd be using the time to close down his organization. That would give us the comfortable feeling—in spite of our anxiety about Clare—that after all, the KGB plot had been thwarted, and even if Vlasov and his minions disappeared the information in our possession would ensure that nothing of the kind could be attempted in the foreseeable future. But as I said just now, Vlasov is desperate. He must save something from the wreckage of his plans. If not, he will undoubtedly face a court-martial in Moscow. So I think he's planning to complete part of the operation tonight, by infiltrating any agents he has already trained into Albania, and at the same time liquidating his base here.'

Ingram nodded approvingly. 'It'd be a neat solution to the security problem, too. He's got that big motor yacht still, I suppose, the one he used to pick up Spiro and me. He could dump his agents in the sea off the Albanian coast, go back to his base, and evacuate all his Corfu personnel to some hideout in the Greek mainland. There'd be no one left for the SB men to put the screws on.'

Jenny looked puzzled. 'But if he releases Clare tomorrow there's nothing to stop us from telling all we know about the operation.'

'If,' put in Ingram grimly, 'we're alive to do it.'

'Exactly,' said Grant. 'That's what we've got to face. If this line of reasoning is right, Vlasov has no intention of either releasing Clare or letting us get away with out lives. He just wants us three to do nothing at all until he's ready to deal with us. That's why we can't afford to be passive, even if it means taking risks we wouldn't otherwise consider, for Clare's sake. Do you agree, Jenny?'

'Yes. It makes sense.'

'Roger?'

Ingram thought for some time. Then he said quietly, 'We've no alternative. We've got to attack.' He laughed shortly. 'I'm all for attack, now, but just tell me where.'

Inwardly, Grant breathed a sigh of relief. Stage One was over. At least there was consensus among them. He got up from his chair and went over to the wardrobe. 'I've got a bottle of duty-free Glenlivet,' he said. 'And if you'd both get your tooth-glasses we'll have a drink and make a plan of action.'

As Grant poured the whisky into Ingram's glass he said, 'For the sake of efficiency I think one of us had better be in charge.'

'Then it's you, Luke,' said Jenny quickly.

'Roger?'

'I'll go along with that, but before we start planning action I'd like to draft a full report describing what's happened. I'll also write a letter to Jenny's boss in Athens and send them both to the vice-consul under seal, with a cover note asking him not to open it until tomorrow morning, but then take the contents to Athens Embassy by plane. Then, if we're all three knocked off at least we'll get the report into the right hands.' He turned to Jenny and said, rather formally, 'I'd be glad if you'd help me with the drafting. It's got to be a complete report, but as concise as possible.'

'I'd be glad to,' said Jenny. 'But how do we get it into the V-C's hands? Post it?'

'No. One of us could slip the trailers and go to his flat. The office isn't open in the afternoon.'

'I think it's a good idea,' said Grant. 'But before you start working on the report let's just think what other action we could take. So far as I can see, the only possible lead we've got is the name of the man we think must have been drowned last night. Solon Gastouri.'

Jenny picked up the telephone directory and turned the pages. 'That's lucky; he has got a telephone, and his address is 236 Aghios Sofias.' She glanced at Ingram, and added, 'We know the street. There's a little café where we used to have breakfast. It's in the old part of the town.'

Grant said, 'It's a serious risk, but as I said it's our only line. The police may be there, and for that reason Vlasov's people may be giving the place a wide berth. We don't know if Gastouri got away after all; if so, is he in the flat, hiding? If not, is there a wife who might give us some clue to where Vlasov's base is? There are a lot of possibilities, and corresponding risks. I'd have a shot at it myself, but I think it'll have to be you, Roger. You speak Greek fluently, and if you wear sunglasses there's little chance anyone will recognize you.'

'I'll do it,' said Ingram eagerly. 'But I'll need some sort of cover.'

'Take a bunch of flowers,' suggested Grant. 'It's very innocent-looking. If when you get to the flat you don't like the look of whoever opens the door, you can just say you've mistaken the floor, and retreat hurriedly. You'll have the gun, of course, but I hope to God you don't even have to show it.'

Jenny broke in, 'There's a shop just off the Ionian Square, behind the big church, where they sell flowers. I've even seen funeral wreaths in the window.' She turned to Ingram and said laughing, 'I expect some of the flowers on your coffin came from there.'

He looked startled. 'I've scarcely taken in that I'm supposed to be not only dead, but

150

buried. And incidentally,' he added, with a wry smile, 'did either of you produce a floral tribute for that occasion?'

'Bad security,' said Jenny primly, and they all laughed. Oddly, the prospect of action had lowered the tension.

Grant said, 'We're getting somewhere. We now know that two of us have to shake our trailers and visit (a) the V-C and (b) the flat on Aghios Sofias.'

'I'll deliver the letter to the major,' said Jenny.

'If you like. But we're left with a problem— how to slip our leads without making it obvious that we're doing it deliberately. At the same time it's important for us to get clear pictures of the surveillance men, partly to be able to identify them later and partly so that we can assess how many are on the job. My own guess is that Vlasov's forces on Corfu are very thin on the ground. He can't afford a big organization, because as Jenny was saying yesterday, Greeks talk. We may find there's only one trailer attached to each of us, and that they don't want to be spotted for that very reason. I know how we can find this out, but it means planning an itinerary for each of us, to be memorized and followed exactly, with time checks at certain points. The idea is that each can help to spot those following the other two, and without appearing to do more than stroll round and look at the sights.'

'That's interesting,' said Jenny. 'I'd never thought of it. There's a street-map in my room. I'll get it.'

Ingram was already sitting down at the writing table. He said, 'Perhaps you two could do that while I get this thing roughed out.'

Jenny brought in the map, and she and Grant spread it out. 'We'll have an early lunch at the hotel,' said Grant, adding with Northern frugality, 'We pay for half-pension anyway. Then I think we'd all better take a short siesta before we start out. We don't know what we may be up against later.'

'There's just one thing,' said Jenny. 'Oughtn't I to tell the V-C what's happened—not just give him the letter and ask him to act as a messenger-boy?'

'Yes, I think you're right,' said Grant, ignoring a protest from Ingram. 'Barnard's an intelligent, active person, and I'd judge that he has a good sense of security. I know he's non-career, but after all he's a regular Army man and he is the Queen's rep. here, so he doesn't have to do what we tell him. It's worth while to get him firmly on our side, so I agree. Tell him the whole story. Ask him to take no action with the police until we say, for fear of endangering Clare. And if,' he added, with a sardonic smile, 'we're not in a position to say anything, because Vlasov's closed our mouths one way or the other, then let him take action at ten tomorrow morning, when Vlasov's ultimatum runs out.'

He saw that Ingram was still unconvinced. 'There are two advantages in briefing the V-C,' he explained. 'One is that if he's already worrying about Clare we can stop him going straight to the police, and upsetting everything. The other is quite simply this: all three of us are in danger, as I said just now, but it's very unlikely that Vlasov can knock us all off at one go. But if he does start something, and even one of us can get to a telephone, it would be an enormous help for Barnard to have all the details of the case to hand, so that he can get the police cracking fast.'

'Yes,' said Ingram. 'That's good reasoning. I'll draft the letter to Barnard accordingly.'


## CHAPTER ELEVEN

The arrangements to deal with Clare, the English trio at the Cavalieri and the messages had all been made during the hours Vlasov spent in Andreas's flat in the old town after his escape from the fort. He'd had some difficulty with his Corfiot head agent, because Andreas had expressed his views in forthright terms on the death of Solon, and Vlasov had been obliged to promise an extra large bonus if Andreas would help to bring off the landing operation that night. When everything was settled Vlasov had driven to the villa on the east coast where, in spite of his sleepless night, there was much to do before he could take a rest. Here, at least, he was safe for the moment.

During the afternoon there was considerable activity at the villa, and, tired as he still was, Vlasov was the driving force. Several of the six Greek infiltration agents who had been immured there for the past month were smarting from the verbal lashings Vlasov and his assistant Alexei Nikitch had been administering. All of them were of Greek or Greek/Albanian parentage, with the quick wits of the Greek, and they had proved apt pupils in the complicated training sessions. They had learnt how to encode and decode secret messages, how to transmit and receive the signals by ultra high frequency radio, how to repair their sets if they went wrong, how to use secret inks and Minox cameras. They had learned report-writing, the rules of personal security, and the techniques of recruiting clandestine informants. They knew how to make pick-locks and forge keys from a wax impression. Some of them had shown special aptitude for breaking into the old-fashioned safes and strong-boxes which are general in the country districts of Albania. These were the essential skills, the tradecraft, of espionage and secret action. In addition, they had to be briefed, and this was to have been spread over a number of weeks. Now it all had to be done in one day. There was much to memorize, and their nerves were on edge.

Vlasov's plan had been to despatch the men two at a time during late October, when the sea, with luck, would still be calm, with little or no moonlight. Now, they all had to be dropped in a single moonlit night, entering the water at carefully-spaced intervals six hundred yards from the Albanian coast, each man towing a plastic bag with his clothes and basic necessities, and with only a self-illuminating compass to help him find his landing-point. The wet suits and aqualungs would then be buried and each man would find his way separately, travelling only by night, to a specified co-operative farm in Greek-speaking territory.

The cover stories were all similar: 'I ran away from the ... state farm, which lies ... kilometres northeast (or east, etc) of ... town. The Albanian overseer, named ..., had been brutal to me and I struck him back (or killed him). In time I want to get in touch with my relatives at ..., but the police are chasing me and I want to find work for the time being on this farm, throwing myself on your mercy.' The forged Albanian identity cards and labour books would support the story initially, but would be destroyed as soon as, with the help of the local Greek farmers, new ones could be obtained. Once accepted into a community the men would work hard, make friends, and keep clear of all political activity for the duration of the winter. In the spring, contact would be made with them and they would be activated, to begin communicating with bases in Greece by radio, and by this means they would receive their instructions and submit their reports.

The agents had been given big steaks and wine for lunch, but no bread (for flatulence might be dangerous), and afterwards they had been denied their usual siesta and the briefing sessions had re-started, Vlasov and Nikitch taking one man each in turn. It was a long process, and would have to be repeated once or twice before each man was word-perfect, since this was the first time that the cover-stories and operational briefings had been revealed. And, also for the first time, the men were allowed to discuss the way their wages would be paid over—a small pittance to a parent or dependant, paid unattributively each month, and the rest to be held for their return to Greece the following autumn; by which time they would have trained others to take their places.

There was a break for coffee, and Vlasov glanced round at the men, who were making the most of the relief from work. They looked fit enough—hard, lean young men with the clear eyes of perfect health, cheerful and optimistic in the face of the deadly risks the night might bring.

Vlasov was an imaginative man—he would not have been the highly competent intelligence officer he was if his imagination had been less lively—and as he strolled out on to the terrace and looked across the sunlit sea at the frowning, and mountains of Albania he deliberately put himself in the place of one of the men he was sending into danger that night.

There were sharks, of course, but they were rare visitors. The greatest danger in the early stages would be the moon, not only for the yacht (although the mini-radar equipment, to be rigged as soon as it was dark, would give warning of Albanian patrol-launches) but for the swimmer. When he neared the land he could stay submerged until he felt the sea-floor rising below him, but the moment would come when he would have to crawl out on to the moonlit sand, take off his flippers and edge forward into cover. He would lie still, listening, with his heart thumping, for sounds of the shore patrols. Then he would dig a grave for his scuba suit with the light-weight shovel in his watertight pack, cover it over, check with brief flashes of a pencil torch that the site appeared undisturbed, and put on the drab clothes of an Albanian peasant. Then he would find his way forward, using his compass and the map he had memorized so painfully. He had to travel ten miles before dawn—that was an order—and find a place to hide before he could take any rest at all.

He would have rations for three days, but would supplement them with eggs and vegetables stolen from the state farms on his route. Not until he was right into the chosen Greek-speaking area could he allow himself to be seen. Water would be another problem until he reached the foothills and the occasional spring. But he would survive, gaunt, bearded, with boots broken by the rocks, and looking—as he was intended to look—every inch a refugee from the hand of the law.

And finally, the acid test. When the infiltrator had reached his target area he would first cache his pistol, radio, and other secret equipment, and then select his first human contact, man or woman, and make his approach, hoping that his halting Albanian would not have to be used and quaking with fear that the family he had chosen might be that of a tax inspector or a rural policeman. Worse still, a party commissar.

He would do all this not for any ideological reasons, but for cash: money waiting for him at the completion of his mission, money that would provide food, drink, girls and a life of ease—until the next time.

It was bad security, thought Vlasov, to let them all know each other, even by pseudonym, because of the danger of interrogation. Most Greeks had heard talk of the Byzantine tortures practised by the Albanian Segurimi—the bastinado, the 'waistcoat' that crushed a man's body to pulp—and it was unlikely that any of the agents would withstand them for long. But none could reveal exactly where any of the others would land, and they had all sworn, crossing themselves in the Orthodox way, that rather than fall into the hands of the Segurimi they would swallow the L tablets that Nikitch had issued to them, and die quickly.

The wind from across the straits suddenly felt chill, and Vlasov shivered and went indoors.

## CHAPTER TWELVE

The object of the exercise that Grant, with the help of Jenny and the street map, had devised during the morning, while Ingram was still struggling to complete his report, was to enable all three of them to assess and identify the Vlasov team which would be following them as soon as they left the hotel. Armed with this knowledge it would be easy for Ingram and Jenny, later, to slip their tails without appearing to do so, and carry out their respective missions. The spot-the-watcher exercise depended on a piece of counter-espionage lore that needs explanation.

If you are being followed by a skilled surveillance team you won't notice them. You stop to look into a shop window, and the man or woman following you walks straight past to the next corner, while another, on the opposite side of the street, casually crosses the road and is ready to follow close behind you when you move on. Another fills the place on the opposite sidewalk. It takes at least three to do the job properly, and if you suspect you're under observation, and adopt evasion tactics, it will require six. But to someone who follows behind the trailers, and knows what to look for, *the whole operation will be as clear as day*. He will quickly spot the trailers as they change positions, move up, move back, cross the street and wait behind corners.

If there is only one trailer, which is rare, it is a little more difficult to spot him, because there is no changing of position. But what soon becomes apparent is the relationship between the target's movements and those of one person—and one only—among the pedestrians following him. The target turns round, and so does the shadow twelve paces behind; the target turns a comer, and the shadow quickens his pace and peers round it, to see if his quarry has continued walking, or has dived into a shop to evade surveillance.

It had been decided that they would start the operation at three o'clock, when they hoped to have heard news on the radio about Solon and the police enquiries into his disappearance. There was ample time for the preparation of the itineraries and schedules, and when they had synchronized their watches it was Ingram who left first. He spent a few minutes wandering along by the balustrade overlooking the sea and then, quickly checking the time, crossed the gardens to Kapodistriou and turned right, just as Grant emerged from the hotel and saw a man in a light jacket and brown slacks, who had been sitting on a bench, fold up his newspaper and cross the road in Ingram's wake. When Ingram stopped to look into the window of one of the tourist agencies the man slowed down. Ingram went on, and at the Voulgareos crossing turned left. Light jacket followed. Grant thought, first blood. Roger's tail identified. He watched as he stood at the intersection, but there was no other trailer. He went into the tobacconist's on the corner and took some time looking at cigars. He bought a packet of Athenes and was standing at the entrance, choosing postcards, when Jenny went past, on the other side of the road, and wandered slowly up Kapodistriou, looking into shop windows.

Grant took his time, paying for his purchases and getting his lighter filled, before he began to follow her, and when she turned into Nikiforou Theotoki he remained about thirty yards behind. There was no doubt now; she had only one follower, and he was trying hard not to be identified.

There was a newspaper shop a little further along the street and here Jenny stopped; she was glancing through a copy of *Paris Match* when Grant caught up with her. He greeted her casually and they looked at the magazines for a moment before he said quietly, 'There's only one—small, dark suit and tie, black moustache, stopping at the leather shop behind me. You can lose him now, and go to the V-C's. Good luck.' He waved his hand and crossed the street without looking round.

The timing was working out as he had hoped, since they had given themselves plenty of slack, to fill in with window-shopping or visits to churches along their respective routes. They were, in fact, doing just what Vlasov had told them to do, acting like tourists.

Ten minutes later, at exactly three twenty-four, Grant was again at the Voulgareos intersection, knowing that Ingram would not have him in sight. He went a little way down Voulgareos, looking at shops, then quite openly consulted his watch, turned, and made his way to the third café under the Liston arcades. He ordered coffee, and a few minutes later Ingram joined him. He had an evening newspaper in his hand, and said, in a low voice, 'They've found the body and identified it as Gastouri's. The address is given, too. I'm afraid it means Vlasov's mob will be keeping away, but not the police. Which may make it difficult for me.'

'Pity. But it's possible they've been and gone. I only hope the widow—if there is one—

is there when you call. Incidentally, you've only got one man after you. Light jacket, brown trousers, canvas shoes, and a newspaper in his hand. About thirty-five, five foot seven and medium weight.' He added a description of Jenny's follower. 'I've told her to shake him and get on with her task.'

'Good. I'll be thankful when that report's safely delivered. But I don't like leaving that part of the operation to Jenny. She might make a balls of it, you know. '

'She won't. That's your man now, behind the tree, under the blue umbrella. The one who's watching the cricket.'

Ingram looked through the archway. Across the road, tables were arranged under the trees, and he saw the man who answered Grant's description. He was just sitting down, with his face half-turned towards the cricket ground, where a team of schoolboys were playing a scratch eleven from an older age group.

'They're quick,' said Grant, as a shout of triumph arose, followed by a round of decorous clapping from the onlookers. A small dark boy in grey shorts had collected a fast drive and thrown down the wicket just as the batsman was reaching for the farther crease. 'Well, Roger. This is the end of the counter-surveillance exercise. We know they've only one follower for each of us, unless there's more than one attached to me—and that doesn't matter because I've nothing to hide.

163

We also know they don't want to be identified, which may mean, as I suspected, that Vlasov really is short of operatives, or needs all he's got for his operation tonight. If that is what he's planning. Are you ready to go?'

'Yes. Wish me luck, Luke. I'll need it. What we want now is a real break.'

*     *     *

Jenny left the bookstall and walked on down the Theotoki to Ionian Square. On her left was a modest one-storey building with dingy stucco walls. An Orthodox priest, his grizzled beard flowing over his black robe, his hair curled up round the base of his stove-pipe hat, was just going in at the door. Jenny followed him and found herself in a sort of ecclesiastical lumber-room, with odd benches, processional banners, a wooden bier and some man-high painted candlesticks stacked around on the dusty boards. The priest was chatting to an old man, the verger probably. She passed them to reach a doorway and moved aside a leather curtain that screened the entrance to a small, dimly-lit church. Candlelight glistened on the gold and glowing colours of the altar screen. The oval face of the Virgin gazed, serene and melancholy, from a silver-encrusted icon at an old woman kneeling at her feet.

Jenny skirted the rows of chairs towards a door on the opposite side of the church. It must lead to the small street running parallel to Theotoki. If her shadow knew of this other door he would be afraid to wait outside in case she should use it to disappear into the maze of small alleys beyond. He was in an awkward spot, as she had planned.

She knelt down, and waited. After a moment or two the leather curtain was pushed aside by a man wearing a dark suit, black-moustached. With bowed head he moved towards the back of the church, and Jenny heard a chink, as a coin dropped into the box. He was following the local practice and selecting a candle. Now he would be lighting it, ready to fix into the rack.

Jenny got quietly to her feet, slipped through the door beside her, and once outside broke into a run, rounded the corner of the little church and turned back into Theotoki. She returned to the church through the door she had first entered. The priest and the verger looked at her, mildly astonished. With trepidation, she lifted aside the leather curtain. The man had gone; the old woman still knelt before the ikon. This time Jenny made for a dim corner at the back of the church and stood with a newly-bought candle in her hand, ready to light it if anyone appeared.

Minutes passed, and the curtain did not move nor did anyone come through the other door. The man was evidently combing the alleys. It was time to move, in case he decided to come back. She walked out of the main door and turning left, made a wide detour, approaching the house where the vice-consul had his flat from the opposite end of the street to the one she would normally have used. No one followed her.

She rang the bell, and a maid answered the door.

'Please tell Major Barnard that I've come from Mr Grant, whom he met yesterday, and that it's very important.' She gave the woman her official Embassy visiting card.

She was shown into the living room and after a minute Barnard appeared, a little testy, since he had been enjoying a long siesta. 'Couldn't this have waited until tomorrow morning, Miss Otfield?'

'I'm afraid not. It's a very urgent matter, Major Barnard, and I had to speak to you personally. May I sit down?'

'Oh, er—yes, of course. What's this message from Grant? Can you make it fairly brief? I have an engagement in half an hour.'

'All right, then, in a few words. Roger Ingram is alive.'

The major's face flushed ominously. 'I don't appreciate that kind of joke. I was present when he was buried.'

'The man found by the police was someone else. Mrs Ingram was forced to pretend it was her husband, who in fact had been kidnapped by KGB agents. He is free now, and I was with him only an hour or two ago. He's written this letter to you, with a report on the whole affair.'

The vice-consul drew half-glasses from his breast pocket and took the four sheets of Cavalieri writing paper, still disbelieving. But as he read his manner changed, and his shaggy eyebrows rose alarmingly. His first reaction was official. 'That this should happen on my— er—patch,' he growled, 'is the most disgraceful thing I've ever heard of. Who do they think they are, these bandits? I must tell the police at once.'

He was reaching for the telephone when she stopped him. 'That would result in Mrs Ingram being killed, Major, to remove the evidence. You saw that her husband made that point most strongly in his statement.'

'Yes, I suppose so.' He walked to the wall and rang a bell, and when the maid appeared ordered tea with rum. 'I think we could both use a stiffener,' he said. 'And now please explain how you come into this, and how on earth Mr Grant is involved. As far as I know he's a perfectly bona fide Foreign Service officer, and it's no concern of his, all this espionage business. If anyone is to help, it's my job.'

'He's an SIS officer,' said Jenny, 'and so of course is Roger Ingram. And so am I. But we must if possible keep that fact from the Greeks; otherwise it would put the ambassador in an awkward position.'

167

Barnard's old eyes twinkled. 'So you're a licensed spy, are you? A sort of Jennifer Bond.' He chuckled heartily at his little joke, but stopped when he saw the look in Jenny's dark eyes. She evidently was not amused. 'All right, my dear, I realise how serious this matter is. But I want to get it straight in my mind. So would you please tell me the whole story, from the beginning?'

The tea-tray came in when she was half-way through her explanation, and the major took the silver teapot, poured out two cups and added slices of lemon and generous measures of Greek rum. Jenny drank gratefully, and went on.

When she had finished Barnard was silent, thinking. 'The trouble is,' he said at last, 'that even if we could tell the Astinomion Polion it would only put them into a flat spin. They aren't geared for this sort of thing, and their first reaction would be to radio Athens for a Special Branch squad to help them sort it out. And I'm afraid tongues might wag; it's too exciting a story to keep quiet—you know what Greeks are. And then this Vlasov would find out and—as you said, young lady—remove the evidence. No, the only people who could really snap into action are the naval intelligence lot at Kassiopi. They could at least stop any shipment of spies to Albania, as it's part of their job to keep watch on the traffic in the straits. But they'd have to know roughly where the chaps would be despatched from.'

'And in the meantime Mrs Ingram would be at the mercy of Vlasov and his gang,' said Jenny.

'Yes, I agree. So what can Grant and Ingram do? I suppose they've decided to toe the line and do damn' all until they get back Mrs Ingram tomorrow, is that it?' There was a slightly contemptuous edge to his voice.

'No, it isn't,' said Jenny sharply. 'For one thing, Luke Grant says he doesn't see Vlasov keeping his bargain. He'll do whatever he's planning, but he won't let go of Mrs Ingram, since she'll still be a guarantee of our silence. So we've got to find some way of releasing her.'

'But that's a tall order, if you don't know where she is.' He looked at her suspiciously. 'Ah, I see you've got a line you won't tell me about, and you and your two dashing friends are planning some sort of commando raid. I took part on one of those once,' went on the major, reminiscing wistfully, 'blackened faces, crawling under wire, sneaking up behind a sentry and strangling him with a nylon cord. I was scared to death, I can tell you. Is that what you have in mind?' He saw her hesitate, and exclaimed, 'God bless my soul! It *is*. In Corfu, of all places.'

'We aren't planning anything of the kind,' said Jenny firmly, annoyed that her face had betrayed her.

'Oh no, I'm sure. But I hope you've got weapons. I gather the other side has, including bombs.'

'I'm afraid,' said Jenny sarcastically, 'it'll have to be the nylon cord. You couldn't lend me one, Major?'

He burst out laughing. 'I like you, young lady, even if you are trying to keep me in the dark. Oh well. As a matter of fact, I've got an old Browning in that drawer.' He went over to his desk, unlocked a drawer and showed her the weapon, gleaming under a film of oil. 'I keep it in good order. You never know what some of these hippies might get up to.' He left the drawer unlocked. 'I'd have liked to lend it to you if you'd really needed it, but of course, in my position that's impossible. Excuse me a moment, will you, my dear. I'll be back in a minute. It's my tropical bladder, y'know,' he added with an apologetic chuckle.

'Bless him!' murmured Jenny, as she checked that the Browning was loaded and slipped it into her shoulder bag. By the time he came back she was sitting on the sofa again, reading Roger's report.

Barnard, who on the other side of the door had heard the distinctive click of the gun's breech, sat down in his chair by the desk. 'Now listen to me, my dear. Go back to those other two and tell them that in view of the situation they're in I'll take no action until tomorrow morning, at ten o'clock, but that they would be

170

most unwise to do anything, in the meantime, that could cause trouble with the local authorities. However, should they chance to find out where that shipment of spies is to be despatched from, if they'll let me know I could ask the admiral at the naval base to see me, and explain the whole situation to him. I'll keep this report of Ingram's on my person, and shall be at the Corfu Club from about six-thirty to eight, then back here for dinner and bed. Now be off with you—and good luck!' He rang for the maid to show her out.

\*　　　\*　　　\*

When Ingram left the table under the Liston arcade Grant went to stand under the trees, a few feet away from the man in a blue pin-stripe suit whom Ingram had identified as Grant's tail. They both watched the cricket match for a short time, and then Grant walked away up the George I towards the Royal Palace. It was a way of keeping at least one of the watchers occupied.

He climbed the broad steps leading up to the magnificent Doric colonnade which forms the entrance to the Palace of St Michael and St George, designed, strangely enough, by a British colonel of engineers. From the terrace he looked back at the cricket ground and gardens of the Esplanade — and the figure of his follower pausing uncertainly near the bottom of the steps. Grant spent half an hour in the Palace, persuading a junior curator to let him see the state rooms where first the British Lords Commissioners and later the Kings of Greece had held their receptions, and which are normally closed to the public. It amused Grant to think that many of his colleagues in the FCO were members of an Order of Knighthood that had been created here in an effort to keep the Corfiot worthies sweet.

His tour of the museum was nearly completed when he looked at his watch and found it was time to meet the others. As he came out on to the terrace he saw that pin-stripe had been joined by the two other surveillance men, and they were talking together under the trees. Bad discipline, thought Grant, but understandable. They had had a frustrating afternoon.

But at least he knew that Ingram had got away without anyone following him. He went down the steps and strode past the three men along the road flanking the Liston. Five minutes later he was in his room at the Cavalieri. Neither Jenny nor Ingram had returned.

*     *     *

Roger Ingram had got rid of his shadow by the simple and natural-seeming method of catching a bus. For a little he waited by the lights at the end of the Liston, looking around as if uncertain where to go. He had seen three buses taking on passengers at the halt by the car-park and guessed that at least one of them would have to stop at the lights. One did, and he rapped on the glass sliding doors and gesticulated at the driver. The man opened the door to let him in—breaking the rules, no doubt, but the Corfiots are friendly people. Looking back, as he paid the minimum fare, Ingram could see his man trying desperately to stop a taxi, but it slid past him. At the next halt Ingram got out and dived into a narrow alley, working round towards the old part of the town near the Orthodox Cathedral of Saint Theodora. In five minutes he had reached the ancient street of Aghios Sofias.

He was wearing dark glasses to avoid a chance recognition, so he could take his time about sizing up No 236. As he passed by on the other side of the street he could see it was an old house of Venetian origin, with the high, arched entrance and the windows of its three storeys framed in marble. The great doors were open, and inside he could see a stone-paved yard from which a staircase curved up to the floors above. Originally, no doubt, the house, on the Italian pattern, had consisted of store-rooms at ground level, a *piano nobile* for the head of the family on the first floor and the rest housing children, relatives and servants in order of importance. Now every floor had been divided into flats, as Ingram saw when he retraced his steps and went into the entrance.

There was a tier of shabby tin letter-boxes, and one of them bore the name 'S.R. Gastouri, 30'. It was empty, possibly showing that someone had cleared it that day. There was nobody around. Ingram dodged back and peered cautiously up and down the street, but it was deserted except for a woman with a shopping bag. He walked quickly to the florist that Jenny had mentioned, and a few minutes later was climbing the dark stone stairs with a bunch of white chrysanthemums in his hand, carefully done up with cellophane and a broad black ribbon. On the third floor a little daylight filtered in through a high window, and he could just read the name 'Gastouri' on a card pinned to the door.

He had a cover-story ready, a little threadbare, admittedly. If a policeman should open the door he would mutter 'For the *Kyría*', and retreat hastily. If the door were opened by anyone else—well, he would play it off the cuff, and for the worst event he had the gun in his pocket.

He grasped the chipped porcelain knob at the side of the door and gave it a tug. As he heard the bell jangling inside his heart seemed to be squeezing against his ribs, but he reminded himself that this was their only lead, and the prize, after all, was Clare.

The tall door swung open and he was faced with a girl in her late twenties dressed in deep mourning, not the traditional black cotton of the Greek peasant woman, but some sort of synthetic material nipped in at the waist and pleated. The girl's make up was smudged with tears, but her expression was challenging, even angry.

In his fluent but accented Greek Ingram offered his condolences. For a moment she stared at him, then broke into a rapid tirade.

'So you've come at last, have you? So you're the foreigner my Soli worked for. You let him die, and you think a few thousand drachmas and a bunch of flowers will make up to me for losing my husband, and the home we were to have, and . . .' The shrill voice paused for a moment.

'*Kyría,*' broke in Ingram urgently, 'the neighbours will hear. Please let me come in and explain.' Uncertainly, she stood back and allowed him to pass into a dark hallway, then opened a door leading to a large room overlooking the street. It was furnished with a plastic-covered suite of strident red, bought, Ingram guessed, from the proceeds of profitable tourist outings in *Hysperia*. A bunch of dyed grasses and paper flowers stood in an orange vase on a shiny table, and there were photographs of a swarthy, handsome man and wedding groups in gilt-wire frames.

She was still talking as she motioned Ingram

175

to sit down, perching herself at one corner of the sofa. She was telling him what a splendid husband Solon had been, such a good provider, a businessman who associated with rich foreigners. If he had lived, how different life would have been. 'But for you,' she added ominously, 'all would be well.'

'*Kyría*,' said Ingram, 'you are mistaken. I am not Solon's boss. I was his friend, many years ago. Perhaps before he met you. We used to go out in his little sailing boat and spend wonderful days together, and he taught me to catch big fish. I would never have wished harm to come to him. When I read of this terrible thing in my newspaper this afternoon my first thought was to come and see you.' He handed her the flowers. She thanked him, left the room and came back with a large china vase into which she crammed the chrysanthemums, and a jug of water on a tray. She crossed the room to the sideboard, poured ouzo into glasses, added water and offered one to Ingram, who bowed his thanks.

He opened his cigarette case and the girl took one and accepted a light, blinking as the smoke stung her eyes, smudging the mascara a little more.

'Tell me, *Kyría*, how this dreadful thing happened.'

'But I don't *know*,' she cried. 'Soli was here, with me, and we were just going to bed when Andreas rang and said the boss wanted to have the doctor's launch—it's one Soli hires when he takes people deep-sea fishing—and Soli was to take him out in it, and he would pay double the usual fee. And it was very important and they wouldn't be away for long; Soli would be back before dawn. And I waited and waited, and he didn't return. I wondered ... Soli was a very handsome man, I thought he'd picked up some ... And I couldn't ring Andreas because I don't have his number. And then this morning they talked on the radio about the *Hysperia*, and of course that was the name of the doctor's boat. The one Solon hires from him. He never uses a small boat now,' she added, with pride.

'And?'

'Then the police came round and—No, it was before that. One of those men came and brought me the money, and said I mustn't tell the police anything, and they'd come and see me again. So when the Polion called I told them nothing—I said I didn't know who Soli had been with. And they said they'd found his body in the sea, beyond the fort, and knew who he was by his fishing licence. But it wasn't just drowning.' Her tears were running freely now. 'They said he must have used dynamite to kill fish—and that's a thing Soli would never do. As if he couldn't catch fish in all the other ways.'

Ingram patted her plump little hand, with its painted finger nails. 'And Solon's boss, the man who took the *Hysperia*, surely he came to see you? It was the least he could do.'

'I wasn't even supposed to know his name. It was Rossi. No, he kept away. But I know where he lives,' she added triumphantly.

'That shows how much Solon trusted you,' said Ingram, containing his excitement. 'If it was all so secret.'

'That's what he thinks,' she said, with a hard little laugh. 'But I know where the house is because Soli took me to see it, one day when *Kyríe* Rossi was away in his big yacht. We went by sea. The villa is right on the water, in a beautiful little bay.'

'I think I know it,' said Ingram disingenuously, and, at a venture, 'It's Koloura, isn't it?'

'No. It's Kalami. Mr Rossi took the villa for five years, but he told Soli that he wouldn't need it that long and when he left, we could use the house for the rest of the lease if we kept some rooms for him. We'd got it all planned, and that's why Soli took me to see it. I was to do the cooking and Soli would take them out in the boat—the guests, I mean.' Her face fell. 'But now Soli is dead, and if Rossi doesn't send me more money I'm going to go to that villa with the police. There's something Soli wouldn't tell me about, that goes on there. I think it's drugs. But perhaps Rossi was killed when the launch hit the bridge, and no one will look after me. I shall be a widow all my life, wearing black.' She sobbed into her hands.

Ingram felt sorry for her and, after all, she had given him just the information he wanted, the place where Clare was being held prisoner. As he said goodbye he added that he would try to find a way of helping her. And he meant it; the Athens station ought to be good for a handsome case bonus, sent anonymously.

There was no one about as he went down the dark stairs and out into the street.

## CHAPTER THIRTEEN

As before, the meeting was to be held in Grant's room. He had washed the tooth-glasses they had used in the morning and set them out, with the Glenlivet and a bottle of water, on the table in the window, when he heard Jenny's knock.

She came in, took off her ethnic shoulder bag and swung it for him to catch. 'Feel what's inside,' she said triumphantly.

He touched the Browning, and felt his fingers close comfortably round the butt. 'Good girl! The V-C, I suppose? You must have used all your feminine guile on the old boy. Was he helpful in other ways?'

'Very. But let's wait until Roger comes, don't you think?'

Grant nodded, and they were sipping whisky

179

when Ingram arrived. 'No need to ask if your assignment went well,' said Grant. 'You look like a cat with a saucer of cream.'

Ingram pulled up a chair and settled astride, his arms on the back. He told his story well. He was a little shame-faced about the manner in which he had worked his way into the confidence of a woman so recently bereaved, but added, 'All the same, she's got her eyes on the main chance. I'm pretty sure that for her, life goes on and what she wants now is to put the bite on Vlasov, alias Rossi, if she can find him, and make him ante-up more cash and maybe the use of the villa as well when his operations are over. Though the story that he offered to let Solon turn the villa into a guesthouse is, of course, a load of codswallop. The explanation, as I see it, is that Vlasov planned, if all went well and he could withdraw from the island for the present, to let Solon act as caretaker and run the place as a sort of resthouse for his operatives. Solon would be there permanently, to maintain radio contact with the mainland—and perhaps Albanian bases as well by then—and to be in a position to despatch any more infiltration frogmen who might be required.'

Grant nodded. 'That's my reaction, too. But what is this place Kalami like?'

'It's the scene of whole pieces of the Durrell books, a small circular bay surrounded by steep, wooded hills. The summer tourist caiques pass it when they make the Kassiopi run, just before they stop at Koloura, round the headland. There is a large white villa at the edge of the water. That must be the one. Otherwise there are only a few small houses amongst the olives. I even know the villa, though I've only seen it from the sea. It used to belong to Bill Paton, an English actor, and he certainly had it last year, so it's quite on the cards that he's leased it to the phony Signor Rossi for five years.

'It's an ideal place for an embarkation base, with water deep enough to moor a big motor yacht right alongside the lower terrace. There was one tied up there when we passed. It would be child's play to guard, too. Any vehicle coming from landward would be seen at intervals as it went down the road which runs from the headland to the shore. And heard as well. You'd get at least three minutes' warning before a police squad could arrive, and in that time a lot can happen. But you and I, Luke, could leave the car right up in the maquis and come down the hill on foot through the trees with hardly any risk of being seen or heard. I feel almost certain that's where Clare is being held. Now we'd better hear what Jenny has to say.'

If Jenny resented the slight air of condescension in Ingram's remark she did not show it. She told her story quickly, and summed up: 'The V-C is a good sort and by no means averse to a bit of action. But obviously he's got to protect his rear as regards both the Office and the local authorities. So we must never let out the fact that he's sitting on information of concern to both. His offer to bring in the naval security people into the action is one we could take advantage of, if other methods fail. Finally, he's doubled our armoury, and we owe him a vote of thanks for that.'

Ingram said, 'It's best to face it. The only way we can release Clare is by doing it ourselves, and God knows we'll be lucky if we can make it.' He pulled a folded map from his pocket and spread it out on the desk. 'Here's Kalami, bang opposite the Albanian coast and about fifteen miles north of Corfu. As I said, we could leave the car here, on the side road, and hide it in the bushes. The turning to Koloura leaves the main road here, and just when it begins to dive down to sea-level a track leads off to the right, makes a turn round the headland and drops steeply down to Kalami. But we could go straight down on foot from the place where we've left the car. With luck there'll be some moonlight, and there should be plenty of cover in the trees. The villa's away to one side, some distance from the other houses, and the slope, covered in trees, almost overhangs the house. So we ought to be able to get there. What happens then—' He shrugged his shoulders, and turned to Grant. 'You said

182

you'd help. Well, will you?'

'I'm sorry,' said Grant, 'but from your description of the place I don't see how we stand a dog's chance of getting into the house and releasing Clare. For all you know they've strung trip-wires round the villa. And as for creeping down a rocky slope, try doing that without setting a few stones rolling, and alerting the guards. There must *be* guards.'

'Then we knock them off,' said Roger impatiently. 'For Christ's sake, Luke, I know as well as you that it's a desperate plan, but I *am* desperate. If what you said is right—and I think it is—then Vlasov is going to take Clare with him when he winds up his operations and clears out. It's the only way he can ensure our silence. But we've now got an element of surprise and, thanks to Jenny's initiative, we've got two serviceable guns.' He looked at the girl for support.

Internally, Jenny was seething, but she said nothing. She was watching Grant's face and realizing, for the first time, that if he went out of her life it would be a loss she would find hard to bear. The contrast between the two men was striking. Roger's thin, mobile face, even disguised by that ridiculous beard, expressed exactly the man's personality—the keen whetted intelligence, the pride and ambition, the passionate drive, the courage, but with something vulnerable: all the things for which she had loved him so dearly, and

183

which could still give her pain.

And the other man so reserved yet strangely perceptive, with a strong male attraction that roused her in spite of herself. He was speaking now, with that half-sardonic twist of his lips: 'You've stuck a gun to my head, Roger, and I've no option, I suppose. You certainly couldn't get anywhere alone, I know that. But if I help you it must be on my terms, and the first condition is that we recce the place slowly and thoroughly, and if I decide we can't succeed, we go back and try something else. And I think I'd better still be in charge.'

Ingram moved his shoulders restlessly. 'There's nothing else we can try and anyway, I'm perfectly capable of—'

Grant raised his voice slightly. 'I said those were my terms, Roger.'

'Oh all right, I agree. I've no option, have I?'

'And what is my part in this scheme?' asked Jenny coldly.

'Oh Jenny,' cried Ingram impatiently. 'Get this straight. You don't have a part. This really is a man's job. I know you've got all the guts in the world, but—'

'Jenny's part,' interrupted Grant firmly, 'is to stay here.' He turned to the girl, anxious to convince her. 'If we're not back here, with Clare, by 1 am we shall have failed. And you'll be in danger, because if Vlasov's nobbled us he'll try to get you, too. What he doesn't know is that Barnard has that statement of Roger's. Nor does he know we've got his base identified. So your role is vital. We'll have to take both guns, so you'll be defenceless. If we don't return by one, ring the V-C, get him out of bed and make him come here so that you can tell him what we've discovered. Then he can get the naval people moving, or the police, or whatever he thinks best. We shall depend on you. Are you quite clear what you have to do?'

'Those are your orders, are they?'

'Yes.'

'I see.' But her eyes were rebellious.


## CHAPTER FOURTEEN

They left the hotel, all three together, scarcely bothering about the men still dutifully trailing after them. Grant had enquired of the desk clerk when the casino in the Achillion opened, and had traced with him the route the car should follow. 'Leave Corfu about half-past eight, and you'll be there in nice time,' the man had said. With any luck, he would pass on his information.

'Let's go to the place in Theotoki where they roast chickens on spits,' said Jenny. 'The smell of charcoal makes one hungry.'

They sauntered along the Kapodistriou, and

Grant felt almost light-hearted now that they had a plan to follow. Difficulties and disappointments—and worse—might come soon enough.

The juicy chicken with its crisp brown skin was delicious, and they ordered more, and took their time over the meal. 'I can't help feeling sorry for our escort,' said Jenny. 'They've been on duty since morning. You were right, Luke; Vlasov hasn't enough men to work shifts. Do you think we should take them some chicken?'

'Oh don't be silly,' snapped Roger. Beneath his casual manner he was still very tense.

'Time to leave,' said Grant. 'Jenny, you go back to the hotel—and stay there. That'll draw off one of the men. Roger, you and I will take a little stroll and try to catch the men off-guard before we pick up the car. How about taking a look at the wreck of the *Hysperia*, if she's still there?'

Jenny went off without a word. The two men walked past the Liston and under the trees beside the car park to the gateway leading to the fortress bridge. It was locked and guarded by a sentry. 'That's quite normal,' said Ingram. 'I forgot that the visiting hours end at seven o'clock. Never mind. We checked the position of the car and it's perfect. Nose on the edge of the drive-in. All set for a smooth and natural-seeming getaway.'

As they drove off they heard the sound of

running steps in the darkness behind them. 'He'll never make it,' said Ingram contentedly. 'We'll circle the town and drive straight to Gouvea, where we join the coast road.'

They reached the coastal highway comfortably aware that they had given the slip to their followers. They could see the calm sea reaching away to where, on the mainland, the low-lying tongue of Greek Epirus finally ended, hemmed in by the frowning mountains of Albania. They passed through the tourist strip of big hotels and neon-lit tavernas, from which they could hear snatches of bazouki music as they went by. Past Dassia, Ipsos and Pyrgi, with the road rising, until the heights of Pantokrator appeared on the landward side, with groves of olives and cypresses giving way to silvery firs on the upper slopes.

'There's too much bloody moon,' grumbled Ingram, but almost as he spoke sheet lightning over Pantokrator showed up the heavy rain clouds gathering around its summit.

The road had swung inland to higher ground, then curved seaward again, and they could see the Albanian coast very near. 'I'd better slow down,' said Ingram. 'The turning's inconspicuous even by daylight, and just now one could easily overshoot.'

The wheels crunched on an unsurfaced road that dipped through the maquis towards the sea. 'Put her in here,' said Grant, pointing to a break in the brush wide enough to take the small car. Ingram edged the Fiat in until its rear was about three feet from the verge, its outlines completely hidden by myrtle bushes.

'Look.' Grant pointed. Below, on the farther side of the bay, lay the villa, white against a mass of trees. The motor-yacht was moored at the lower terrace. Behind it, under the arches which supported the weight of the front of the house, all was darkness. 'We'll strike down from here, bearing right diagonally so as to finish up about half-way to the sea. That'll bring us to the trees, and from there we can drop straight down to the villa.'

The going was not easy. It would have been difficult even in daylight but now, as clouds passed fitfully across the moon, their footholds were uncertain, and they often stumbled over the branches of low-growing shrubs. The harsh, stony ground was treacherous, and on the steep slope stones broke away beneath their feet with a clatter that seemed, in the stillness, alarmingly loud.

Ahead of them lay the woods, like a fur stole flung down on the bare hillside. Under the trees the going was softer, but there were dried branches ready to snap beneath their feet. There might be trip-wires, too.

'Slide your feet forwards,' whispered Ingram, 'so that you push the dead wood aside instead of treading on it. Like that you might feel a wire in time ...'

They had progressed a hundred yards,

nerves stretched, and were straining their eyes for a glimpse of the house and its immediate surroundings when without warning all vision was blotted out as if a switch had been thrown, and as they looked up, startled, at the heavy clouds covering the moon, they heard behind them the seething rush of the oncoming storm. The 3,000 foot bulk of Pantokrator had burst the clouds like bags of water.

Grant had heard of these torrential storms on Corfu, but the reality was impressive even for one used to the devastating rain of the tropics. The heavy drops smashed down on their heads painfully, soaking them to the skin within seconds, absorbing sight and sound. They ran for shelter under the thick foliage of an ancient ilex and huddled against its trunk. The water shed by the branches surrounded them like an unseen curtain of liquid rods, battering down the grass and bushes and spattering both men from head to foot with spray. There was a brilliant flash of lightning and almost simultaneously a deafening crack of thunder.

Grant felt for Ingram's arm and pulled him close, shouting into his ear. 'This is a real break. From inside the house no-one can see or hear us. Let's go on down.' He dived through the curtain of water and the other man followed, bowing his head under the ceaseless, deafening onslaught and groping for the shelter of one tree after another.

Now they could see, by the flashes of lightning, the back of the house, with a short flight of steps leading up to the main door from the path below them. The slope of the hill was so steep that they were on a level with the roof, and Grant realized, from what he had seen above, that the steps must lead to the first floor, probably the main living area of the house. As they watched, a man with a gun, hunched against the deluge, came running along the path and disappeared into the doorway.

The lightning struck again, and again there was the almost simultaneous *cr-r-r-ack* of the thunder. The flash of white light was refracted by the rain, but for a split-second Grant could see a crazy pattern of white shapes appearing among the glistening trees. One was only a yard ahead of him, and he reached forward and felt the louvred side of a large square box. For a moment he was baffled, then smiled as he brought his head forward until it nearly touched the box. Even above the racketing of the storm he could pick up an angry buzzing. The bees were showing their excitement at the pounding of the rain on their roof and wooden alighting board. He felt for Ingram's arm. 'Bee-hives. We'll have to steer clear. If we knock over one of these, rain or no rain, they'll get us.'

They were sliding now, over the battered grass and mud, inching their way between the hives and the tree-trunks. They edged further to the right and waited for another flash. When it came they could see that the path, now a muddy torrent, ended in a little paved platform against the spur of the slope that hemmed in the house on the far side. It was balustraded, and steps led down to terraces on two levels, built out from the side-wall of the villa. But it was impossible to discern more while the flash lasted.

The two men crawled down to the edge of the slope above the path. There were no more signs of life outside the house, which was not surprising, for the rain was still beating down with unabated fury, but there were lights behind the shuttered windows of the upper floors. Grant ran forward, crouched by the balustrade at the top of the terrace steps, and peered over the edge. Ingram followed. There was another flash of lightning, with the thunder following after a tiny pause. They felt naked, silhouetted in their dripping dark clothes against the marble slabs on which they were crouching, but the light was sufficient for them to see a door leading into the house from the middle terrace. It was half-glazed, but there was no light behind it. They ran quickly down the steps and Grant tried the handle of the door. It was locked. Ingram shone his diving torch through the glass and glimpsed a wide passage, empty but for some garden furniture stacked away for the winter.

They went to the edge of the terrace and looked down, waiting for the next flash. It came, but feebler now, and they could see the lowest terrace leading onto the stone quay. Without hesitating, they ran down the steps and took refuge under the arches, their hands on the guns in their hip pockets, alert for a sound, a movement, or even a glint of light. But there was nothing but the slap of water on the hull of the big motor-cruiser they could see beyond the quay, and the sounds of the storm. At the rear of the arcade were double doors, open wide. They went inside and Ingram, shading the lens of his torch with his hand, shone the beam around. They were in a large chamber, vaulted to support the weight of the upper floors. A flight of stone steps across the wall at one end led to the floor above. At the other, coils of rope and cord, some twenty-gallon oil drums, a length of heavy rubber tubing, a hand trolley, and a whole variety of ship-chandler's equipment were scattered around.

Before they could see more they heard a movement on the floor above and the whole place was lit up by a powerful bulb hanging from the vaulted ceiling. Grant and Ingram ran outside and hid themselves, each behind one of the open doors, which they pulled back towards the wall. With relief Grant saw that enough water had spread inwards through the arches to cover their wet footsteps. The light streaming through the door showed clearly the white motor yacht at her mooring, and glinted on the still falling rain.

They heard a man come briskly down the steps, whistling, and move across to the part of the floor where they had seen the drums. There was a squeaking and banging as he wheeled the trolley into position, and then the sound of a drum being rolled over the stones and heaved on to the trolley. This was followed by the grunts of a man exerting his strength and a moment later came a loud clang, as a heavy piece of metal was dropped on to the paving. Finally, something was moved slithering across the slabs, and there were more metallic noises. Grant could not place them.

It was a little time before the man had finished his work. He came to stand in the doorway a few feet from where Grant and Ingram were flattened against the wall, and they could hear him muttering in Greek as he stared out at the falling rain. A moment later he went in, and up the stairs. The light was switched off. They cautiously emerged from their hiding places and went back into the storeroom.

Ingram flashed his torch, and this time they could take stock of the situation in greater detail. The trolley, now loaded with one of the big drums, was placed so that it could be run straight out onto the quay. The man had unscrewed the bung, using the tyre lever he had dropped on the floor, and had attached a petrol pump, worked by a crank handle. The slithering noise was explained by a long piece of inch hose, attached to the outlet pipe of the pump and neatly coiled.

The two men looked at the drum thoughtfully. It would be easy to unscrew the pump and let the petrol run away, but ... Grant went up to one of the other drums and tapped it gently. It was full. Emptying one drum would be useless. The thought of using the petrol to start a fire ran through both men's minds. There would be no danger to the people in the house because they could escape through a door on either of the two levels immediately above, and that might give Grant and Ingram the chance they needed of rescuing Clare—if indeed she was in the house—and thwarting Vlasov's plan at the same time.

It was a tempting idea, and when Grant drew his cigarette lighter from his pocket and pressed the spring, to make sure that in spite of its soaking condition it would still light, Ingram nodded. But then they looked at each other. There is something evil about the act of arson, and they hesitated. Grant signalled to Ingram to illuminate the rest of the room.

On a line of pegs six wet suits were hanging, and little patches of damp on the floor showed they had been used recently. Then Grant's attention was attracted by a heavy door in the rear wall. With the help of the torch they could peer through a barred opening into a second storeroom, hollowed out of the hillside originally, perhaps, to form a wine cellar, but now used for a variety of purposes. On a shelf at the back of the room they could see a row of seven pound tins, with labels in Greek. Grant tried the door, but it was locked. 'What's in the tins?' he asked.

'Honey,' said Ingram. He pointed to gluey drops round one of the lids, where a few insects had stuck and died. 'There's an extractor for separating it, over there.'

'Honey,' said Grant. '*Honey*, Roger! That's the solution.'

'My God, yes! But the door's locked. Wait.' He flashed his torch over the heap of equipment, and found a length of galvanized wire. 'Will that do?'

'It might. Shine your light into the keyhole so that I can see ... OK. It's quite a simple lock. I don't need the torch now. Just keep listening near the steps.'

He had pushed the tip of the thick wire between the door and its jamb so that he could bend it at right angles. Then he withdrew the wire and made another bend further back to give leverage. 'Ready,' he called softly. 'Bring the torch. We'll have to risk someone coming.'

With the help of the light he inserted the pick-lock, felt for the ward and twisted. Twice the bent wire slipped to one side, but then he made firm contact and forced the slide back. With a dull squeak the door opened. Ingram ran into the storeroom and brought out one of the large tins of honey. He was starting to unscrew the petrol pump when Grant stopped him. 'The drum's probably full to the top. Run the hose out to the edge of the quay, while I turn the pump handle a few times.'

This was done, and Grant opened the tin with the flick-knife and carefully poured a good pint of the heavy golden liquid into the drum, which they rocked violently to mix it in.

'Will it work?' asked Ingram doubtfully.

'I think it must. Chemically, it's sugar, and it'll form caramel in the heat and gradually gum up the valves.' He sniffed. The smell of the petrol spilt outside was drifting in through the arches, but there was nothing they could do about it. It was just one of many risks.

The light came on again with dazzling suddenness. Grant pointed to the storeroom which was out of sight from the top of the steps, and they were inside, with the door closed and the honey tin back on its shelf, before they heard footsteps.

The still atmosphere of the cellar was comfortingly warm after the chill of the room open to the storm, and their damp clothes no longer made them shiver. Keeping back from the barred aperture in the door they could look into the brightly-lit chamber without being seen.

They heard the clink of metal, and Vlasov's voice speaking first in Russian and then, with authority, in fluent Greek. One by one, the men appeared. Some, who looked like sailors, were busy helping the divers to fit on their aqualungs, and watching while they tested the gas cylinders. Masks and flippers dangled from their belts. Each man had a large plastic bag, and Grant watched, fascinated, while Vlasov picked on one man at random and made him unseal his bag and display its contents on two upturned barrels for checking. Clothing, a radio set, a long torch, an automatic with a scaled box of ammunition, Albanian money, a compass, ration pack and a folding spade were laid out in turn.

'And the tablets?' asked Vlasov sharply. The man fumbled in the bottom of the bag and pulled out a small aluminium tube.

'Give it to me,' said Vlasov. Fixing his eyes on the man's pale face he unscrewed the top of the tube and shook out two white tablets on to his palm. He put one of these into his mouth and went on talking to the frogman while he adjusted a buckle on his lung harness. Then he took the tablet from his mouth and said, smiling, 'You see, it's quite safe if you don't crush it. But if you do—' Vlasov waved his hand. 'No pain.' The man laughed nervously.

The bag had to be repacked in a certain way, so that its shape was reasonably streamlined and it could be strapped on to the man's back below the gas cylinders.

Someone came into Grant's limited view. Another Russian, by the look of him, and evidently in charge of the details of the operation. He had a clip-board in his hand and talked to each man in turn, smiling, familiar, anxious to keep up spirits—and some of the men looked very tense indeed. They spoke little and fidgeted with their gear impatiently. Some had last minute messages for friends or family, and the Russian patiently noted everything down.

The Greek they had seen earlier went to the trolley and pushed it out through the arches to the yacht. The three sailors followed him.

Vlasov went out to look at the sky and came back with a satisfied expression on his face. There was evidently no sign of a break in the cloud cover. The rain was still falling.

Nikitch had drawn the men up in line, and Vlasov addressed them. He said, 'You are going out on an adventure that few men could be privileged to engage in. It is part of a much larger operation which will, in time, bring relief to your blood-brothers in Albania, now oppressed by hateful tyrants. From other places other teams, like yours, will be entering that country, so you will have friends although, for the time being, you may not meet them. In the old, old times your ancestors, the heroic Greeks of ancient history, invented a means of

198

annihilating their enemies. It was called Greek Fire, and that is the name of this operation of yours. Greek Fire. They used to hurl blazing barrels of naphtha into the opposing ranks from giant catapults, and the barrels burst and spread fire, which ran through the enemy horde and brought terror and death to all in its way. The rebellion you will start will spread like Greek Fire, and it will put an end to the tyrants. I leave you in God's hands.' He crossed himself, in the Orthodox way, and the men, after a moment's silence, broke out into cheers.

'What a charlatan!' muttered Ingram. 'But they fell for it.'

The man with the trolley returned just as the frogmen began to file out into the dark, shaking hands with Vlasov as they went. The two Russians exchanged some remarks in their own language, and then went out, and could be seen now against the lights which had appeared on the yacht, climbing on board and talking to one of the crew. Then Vlasov went ashore, while the other Russian remained on the yacht. A moment later there was a throaty spluttering rumble as the engine started up. There was no doubt about the splutter, but it seemed to recover as the throttle was opened and the yacht moved slowly away from the quay.

Vlasov came hurrying in and stood listening intently for a few moments before he turned away, frowning, and made for the steps. The trolley man followed, and they heard the door above close. The light was switched off.

Grant said, 'The rest of them are probably all in the house, and we don't know where. But at least a sizable number are on the yacht and out of the way for the moment. There can't be many more. If you agree we'll try our luck now. For all we know that stuff may stop the engine entirely before the boat's gone a mile. Do you remember if there was an outboard in reserve?'

'I didn't see one, but it might have been stowed below. I agree we mustn't wait any longer. But Luke—'

'Yes.'

'Our objective is Clare, isn't it? Not Vlasov.'

'Yes. Clare first. OK then, let's go. But we'll need some of that cord.'

They crept up the stairs and listened at the door. There was no sound from within, but the light was on. Grant lifted the latch and pushed the door open.

They came into a broad passage, the one they had seen from the terrace. There was no one in sight. Closed doors on the left. Grant tested the first one. It opened into a large room, unlit. By the light of the torch they could see six camp beds and a few long tables, set with chairs. It was both dormitory and lecture room for the infiltration agents, apparently. The second room, equally dark, housed the canteen, with a television set facing a number of folding chairs, and at one side a serving counter with a bottlegas stove. The smell of garlic and olive oil lingered on the air.

They had reached the middle of the passage when they heard the sound of rushing waters. A door opened and the trolley man appeared, zipping up his jeans. They had had the advantage of a couple of seconds' knowledge that he would be emerging from the door, and they had to silence him. The butt of Ingram's automatic struck the man's head before he could utter a cry. It was a hard blow, and he crumpled and fell slackly to the floor. They pulled him quickly into the lavatory and closed the door behind them. He was trussed up with the cord Grant had brought with him from the storeroom, and they tore off part of his shirt and bound it in place as a gag. Then they propped him on the seat and tied him, still unconscious, to the cistern pipe, so that when he came to he would not be able to attract attention by kicking the door. Ingram removed the key, and they locked the man in.

Outside, the two men exchanged tight smiles, in which there was no complacency, but merely a recognition of their ability to work together in a crisis. They moved silently to the staircase, which brought them out to the entrance hall on the first floor, with several doorways and another stair leading to the bedrooms above. This part of the accommodation was more 'representational', with polished terrazza flooring, newly-painted walls in eggshell grey and shaded ceiling lights.

Grant whispered, 'She could be on this floor or in one of the bedrooms. In either case this is our escape route.' He went softly to the entrance door and slid back the heavy bolts.

Ingram nodded. He approached the door in the middle of the wall opposite the entrance and listened at the key-hole. Then he started violently, and turned to Grant, his eyes blazing with excitement. 'She's in there,' he whispered hoarsely.

Before Grant could stop him, Ingram twisted the knob and thrust the door open.

It was a big room, with the impersonal furniture of a house used for letting. Tall windows faced towards the sea, and at one end an open door gave a view of a study, with a desk covered with papers. Vlasov was standing in one of the windows, looking out into the night, and Clare sat in an armchair nearby wearing dark slacks and a mohair sweater.

Everything seemed to happen at once. As Grant, cursing Ingram's impetuosity, ran past him with his automatic pointing he shouted, 'Hands on your head, Vlasov, *now*!' The man had turned quickly, but at the sight of the gun he slowly raised his hands.

Ingram had no eyes for anyone but Clare, who had sprung from her chair and rushed to meet him—right across Grant's line of fire.

Vlasov's reaction was the swiftest Grant had ever seen. He threw himself forward and got an arm round Clare's waist, pulling her back, while his other hand found the gun in his shoulder holster. He said, 'Drop your pistols, or I'll blow her spine apart.'

'If you did that,' said Grant, 'you wouldn't survive her by a second, and you know it.'

Ingram's eyes were on Clare's agonised face. 'For God's sake,' he entreated, 'don't fire. He'd do it.'

'Of course I would,' said Vlasov tersely, 'and still put you both down.' He drew Clare's body closer, with his face pressed to the fair hair that had tumbled loose. 'I've got a shield—haven't I, my lovely? And you haven't. I'm giving you a chance for your lives, Grant.'

'Roger,' pleaded Clare, 'do as he says.' Ingram dropped his gun, and after a moment's irresolution Grant did the same, tasting to the full the special bitterness of defeat when victory had seemed so close. But he knew he had no alternative now. Vlasov's body was completely covered by Clare—she was almost as tall as he was—and he could pick off either Ingram or Grant at will. Living, each of them was a menace to his plans, and he had shown he had no scruples about killing.

Behind them, the door opened and one of the Greeks appeared. He wore a short apron tied round his waist, and seemed to have come straight from the kitchen, since he was wiping his hands on the apron as he came in. Vlasov spoke to him, and he crossed the room and picked up the two guns. Only then did Vlasov release Clare who, apparently unaware that she had just spoiled a desperate bid to set her free, ran into Ingram's arms.

'Very touching,' said Vlasov to Grant. He took out a handkerchief and wiped his face. 'But she'll get damp and grubby if she twines herself round him like that. Dear me, how wet you both are. Drowned rats, I think you'd say.' Something seemed to strike him, and he uttered a short bark of laughter. 'That has given me an idea,' he continued, in his almost faultless English. 'And it is a good one. Yes, my friends, you may find yourselves a lot wetter before the night is over. Sit down, with your backs to the wall, and Mrs Ingram, please come back to this chair.' Clare didn't move, but clung to Ingram.

'Don't disobey me, madam,' said Vlasov sharply, his voice rising. 'Do as you're told.' She released Roger and walked slowly back to the armchair. 'You'll remember that when I had to discipline you earlier you didn't like it at all.' She collapsed into the chair, and hid her face in her hands.

Ingram was nearly choking with rage. 'You sod! he cried, taking a step forward. 'If you've hurt her I'll kill you.'

'It doesn't show,' said Vlasov calmly. 'Which I'm sure is what matters most to this lady. And you won't kill me, Ingram. Just count yourself lucky if I don't kill you. Now sit down. That's better.' He perched himself on the arm of the sofa. 'Both of you listen to me carefully. I'm sparing your lives for two reasons, although it would give me a lot of pleasure to terminate them painfully. You've caused me enough trouble already. One reason is the old convention that between intelligence services dog doesn't eat dog, although a painful bite may be called for from time to time. The other is that I have just thought of a most attractive way in which I can discredit utterly any account of my Albanian operation which you may somehow have reported to your Head Office. You see, I don't forget that little Miss Otfield is still at large, though not, I hope, for long.'

Internally, Grant groaned. What had the man devised for Jenny? Vlasov was savouring his triumph, and planned to prolong it. He spoke almost genially to the cook, who was holding the two automatics in a most unprofessional manner, and the man laid them on a table near the window and left the room. A few moments later he came back with a new bottle of vodka, misty from the refrigerator, and four glasses. He filled them and passed two to Vlasov and Clare and then, at a word from Vlasov, gingerly set down the other two where Grant and Ingram could just reach them. They were eight feet from Vlasov, but he had his automatic in his hand while he tossed down his vodka at one swallow.

He said, 'Drink it. You may be glad of it later.' Grant drank, and felt the clean bite of the spirit warming his stomach.

'But first,' said Vlasov, 'I think I'd better have you searched.' He gave an order, and the cook went out and returned with two Greeks armed with Schmeisser sub-machine guns. One of them was Kellezi, the Albanian whom Grant and Jenny had left tied up on the Pelekas road the previous day. He gave Grant a vengeful look, and grinned in a way Grant did not like at all.

While the other man covered both with his gun, Kellezi searched them one after the other. As he ran his hand down Grant's leg he felt the shape of the flick-krife, which Grant had thrust into his sock, and drew it out with malicious satisfaction. He passed it to Vlasov, who stood looking down at it thoughtfully while the search was concluded. The guards retreated a few feet, with the muzzles of their weapons still covering the two men.

Vlasov pressed the spring, and the knife whipped out, gleaming evilly. He took a quick stride to where Clare was sitting and grabbed her fair hair from behind, pulling her head against the back of the armchair. With the other hand he held the knife-point at her throat.

'Stop it!' Ingram was frantic. 'You're
206

frightening her.'

Vlasov laughed. 'I'm going to do a lot more than that if you put a foot wrong, either of you. Let me make this quite, quite clear before I go further. If you fail to do exactly as I say this charming lady is going to suffer, and in front of your eyes.' He looked at them thoughtfully, and went on, 'But if you conform—and it won't be easy—she will be well looked after. As now, for example. She's had quite enough unhappiness for the moment, so she may go back to her bedroom and lie down.' He spoke to the second guard, who took Clare out of the room.

Vlasov went back to his perch on the sofa-arm and held out his glass to Kellezi for more vodka. He knocked back the spirit as before, in one gulp, wiped his mouth with his handkerchief, and spoke.

'The first thing you are to do, Grant, is to telephone Jennifer Otfield. I want to find out first whether she's at the Cavalieri, so I'll ring the hotel and ask for her room. If she is there you will speak, and tell her you've succeeded in rescuing Mrs Ingram and add that you want her to take a taxi and meet you at the Koloura turning. (I know you must have come here in your hired car, and that Miss Otfield was not with you when you drove out of the carpark). So that is what she has to do. Explain that your car's brakes have failed. It often happens here.'

'You can't expect me to set a trap for her,' said Grant coldly.

'But that is just what I do expect, and why I had to make it so clear what would happen if you disobeyed me.' He was still fingering the knife.

'I'll do it,' said Ingram in desperation. 'If you won't, I will.'

'No,' said Grant, 'it'd better be me.' He knew neither he nor Ingram had more than a bare chance of surviving the night, but he was damned if he was going to be the cause of Jenny's death, too. It was a golden opportunity to give her a warning and blow the whole Vlasov operation sky-high, whatever happened to him and Ingram. What was more, he might have a chance of getting away with it, if he phrased his words carefully. In any case, he would be standing at the table, some way from those Schmeissers, and Vlasov would be near, to make sure he didn't double-cross. So there was the chance that he could make a dive for the Russian before the guard opened up. These thoughts fled through his mind as he slowly got to his feet and went to the table. The other guard had not returned, which was something.

Vlasov was hesitating. He said, 'Now get this straight. You will say only what I told you, and you will address her by her Christian name, Jennifer, if that's what you would naturally do. I don't know what stage of intimacy you've reached with her, but don't pull any fast ones, Grant. You know what to say?'

Grant nodded. Vlasov had given him one slender straw to grasp at. If he called her Jennifer she should know there was something wrong. If she reacted, he would just bring in 'Jennifer' again, and that ought to clinch it. If not, he would shout a warning and make his spring. His heart began to thump as Vlasov picked up the telephone and dialled with his left hand, with the other holding the gun pointing at Grant's ribs.

He heard the girl on the hotel exchange answering, then a pause, and then a short sentence in Greek. Vlasov replied, and there was a longer pause, obviously while Jenny's name was being paged. But the result was again negative.

Grant, understandably, felt dizzy with relief. Ingram said caustically, 'If you expect either of us to know where she's got to, Vlasov, you're wasting your time. All I can tell you is that the girl has disobeyed orders. She was to stay at the hotel.'

'A pity,' said Vlasov. 'It would have been simpler to get her into the corral as well, but I can try again later. In the meantime, let me tell you my story.' He chuckled. 'Are you sitting comfortably? Then I'll begin. That's what they used to tell children on the BBC, I remember. I once used the phrase for a cypher. All right.

To remind you, I said I had no wish to kill either of you, but that if you wanted to escape with your lives you'd have to help me.

'As I also told you, I have no illusions about the overall security of my operations. You had several hours of freedom in which to send a report to England by post, or confide in someone in Corfu. My task is to throw doubt on your whole story. Let's see. Supposing you, Ingram, have succeeded in getting your report through to London, what will they do with it? What happens in Albania isn't their concern, of course, but they may think to throw a spoke into our wheel by informing NATO, or the Albanians, or both. This would be very embarrassing for me, and my operations would have to be curtailed or abandoned entirely. Am I keeping your attention?'

The two men stared back at him, without a word. He went to the vodka tray and poured himself another glass. He drank, and turned to face them, smiling complacently. 'So what I plan to do is this. When my yacht returns, which will be quite soon, you will both be taken aboard and dressed in the scuba suits used by my instructors. We shall wait until there is no Albanian patrol in the area we've chosen—the boat has an efficient radar, and I expect it's a patrol that's delaying its return now—and shall then run in close to the Albanian coast and dump you overboard.' He chuckled. 'Ah, you say, then we'll swim back to

Corfu; it isn't too far. But you won't be able to, my friends, and for three good reasons. First, you will have no flippers. Secondly, there will be empty oxygen cylinders secured to your backs in such a way that even with each other's help you won't be able to get rid of their weight in the water. However, you will survive, because you'll be near enough to the coast to reach it, just. But by that time, owing—and this is the third good reason—owing to an injection you will be given before you enter the water you will be feeling very drowsy. In fact, all you'll be able to do is crawl out of the sea and fall asleep. And that's how the shore patrol will find you tomorrow morning.'

'It's clever,' said Grant, playing for time.

'It's brilliant, because it has a fail-safe factor. If you fall asleep too soon, and drown, your bodies will still be found, with all the damning evidence. What will the Albanians think when they find two British subjects who have apparently failed to penetrate their defences? After all, it wouldn't be the first time your Intelligence Service has tried to infiltrate agents into Albania. They will make it a *cause célèbre*. Your chance of getting a visit in prison from any compatriot will be nil. Your country has had no diplomatic relations with Albania since 1946. By the time the protecting power—it's the Swiss, isn't it?—takes up your case you will have spent many weeks in a rat-infested Albanian gaol, and I shall have

211

liquidated my commitments here. If you did succeed in passing on Spiro's information, or should Miss Otfield escape from the little trap I shall set for her, no one is going to take your revelations seriously—least of all the Albanans.'

He was smiling triumphantly, delighted with his own cleverness, when he glanced at his wristwatch, and immediately his expression changed. He looked aghast. Absorbed in his argument, he had taken no note of the passing of time; that was obvious to the two men watching him. Vlasov turned to the window and stared out into the darkness. But there was no sign of the yacht. He stood for a moment, frowning, and then went quickly into his study, with a word to Kellezi, and closed the door.

'Bad security,' observed Grant, glancing sideways at Ingram. 'He's going to break radio silence. Something's gone wrong with the yacht,' he added, for Kellezi's benefit.

Ingram took his cue. He laughed up at the man who stood facing them, with his sub-machine-gun pointing at each in turn. 'Your friends aren't going to get anywhere tonight,' he jeered, 'except maybe back here.'

'Be quiet,' growled the man. 'No talking.'

'Did you find your money, Kellezi?' asked Grant, deliberately provocative. 'You must have looked pretty silly, chasing around like a butterfly-hunter. But you couldn't find that receipt for the petrol you bought on Paxos, could you? That's what gave the game away.'

'*Be silent!*' said Kellezi, but his tone was less confident. 'I order you. No more words.'

'We take no orders from a rat who'll betray his country to the Russians,' said Grant slowly and distinctly. He leant back against the wall.

The man's face was contorted with fury. He raised the gun, but fearful of Vlasov changed his mind. He grabbed the knife and flicked out the blade, looking down at it lovingly. 'My knife,' he gloated, as he crossed the room and stood over Grant. '*Your* turn.'

It was a foolish move, but the Albanian was beside himself with rage. He was cradling the Schmeisser in his left arm as he lunged down suddenly with the knife. The sole of Grant's foot caught him in the crotch with such force that it lifted him off his feet. He gave a squeal of agony and dropped the gun, pressing both hands to his groin as he fell.

Grant was trying to extract the Schmeisser from under the man's body when a bullet snarled past his ear. Ingram, who had been reaching for the guns on the table, froze with his hand still outstretched. Vlasov was standing in the study doorway, an automatic in his hand.

'Get back against the wall, both of you,' he said coldly. He came forward, ignoring the moaning Albanian. 'I'll let him have his revenge in a moment, when he's recovered. In

213

the meantime, which of you sabotaged the yacht's engine?'

'Neither of us,' said Ingram. 'It must have been one of your precious agents. They didn't seem to have much enthusiasm for the operation when we saw them going aboard. I expect you've got a mutiny on your hands.'

As he spoke, the sound of a boat's engine came across the water, moving in at slow speed, with a faultless rhythmic beat. Vlasov heard it too, and laughed in sheer relief. Ingram's face was grim. Their plan had failed, he thought. The frogmen would by now be half-way to the Albanian coast, and in a few minutes the crew of the yacht would land and add to their problems.

He and Grant were facing the window, and now they could see the lights of a vessel approaching the quay. Kellezi was standing still half doubled-up but tense, waiting for Vlasov's signal to start work on Grant.

Suddenly, Vlasov's body was outlined against a blaze of light. He swung round and was blinded for a moment by a searchlight shining full on the house facade. At the same moment the door burst open and a man in a naval commando blouse covered the Russian with a sub-machine-gun.

Vlasov whipped round, fired instinctively, and missed. There was an answering burst from the gun, and his body slumped to the ground. Kellezi, who had been balefully stropping the blade of his knife on his thumb, dropped it with a clatter, and raised his hands.

The room seemed to have filled with men in uniform. One of them, in battledress, with three stars on his shoulders, saluted and introduced himself. 'Captain of Marines Protopapas. We've got the men on this floor and the one below. Is there anyone upstairs?'

'My wife,' said Ingram, as he got to his feet. 'I'll go and find her.' He ran out of the door.

'His wife?' said Protopapas, puzzled. 'Ah yes, of course. Miss Otfield mentioned her, but thought she would be on the yacht.'

*Jenny?*' Grant was startled. 'Miss Otfield? Where is she, then?'

'On the patrol launch, sir, just coming alongside the quay. With Commander Metaxa, who is in charge of this operation. My job is the shore-party, you see.' So she had got into the action after all, the little devil. Grant picked up Kellezi's knife from the floor. Perhaps it was just as well, he thought, that she had disobeyed orders.

## CHAPTER FIFTEEN

Jenny was already disobeying orders when, instead of going back to the Cavalieri, she went to a café on the Liston, discouraged the tentative advances of two young Corfiots on

215

the make, and settled down with coffee and brandy to think out her problem. She had chosen a room inside the building where there was an Edwardian wealth of polished wood and heavy upholstery. The drinks were much more expensive here than on the open terrace, but the atmosphere was warm and cheerful. It was a favourite spot for the élite of Corfiot society.

She resented being left out of the two men's crazy plan to storm the Kalami villa and rescue their distressed maiden. What was more, she felt that Roger, at least, had forgotten the prime objective, which was to stop an infiltration of Soviet agents into Albania. All he wanted to do was to find some way of releasing Clare, and Grant, her Luke, had taken a cannot-let-the-poor-chap-down attitude and gone along with him. They were a couple of male chauvinists—or put it another way, just men, who needed saving from their own folly.

Roger had produced various reasons for going it alone, and not bringing in the local authorities: that they would be too slow, that they would be bound to leak information, which would get to Vlasov, with fatal results for Clare—Jenny smiled wryly; the thought had its attractive side—and finally, that once the Corfiot police were brought in Roger and Jenny would have to admit to being spies, and this would embarrass the Embassy. But if

Roger and Luke did somehow succeed in freeing Clare, and even sabotaging the Vlasov operation, how could they explain Roger's reappearance, alive, without the whole facts coming out?

The proper thing to have done was to alert the Greek Navy, and tell someone in authority the whole story. The situation could be saved, Jenny decided, if she herself could put the case to the right person, and make sure that any measures taken did not prejudice whatever action her menfolk might be engaged in at the villa. If things went wrong as a result, well, it would be her fault, and she would resign quickly before they could sack her.

She rang the vice-consul from the café, and rather to her surprise—for he was apparently just finishing dinner—he told her to stay where she was and wait for him. Ten minutes later he appeared, neatly dressed in a dark suit, white silk shirt and regimental tie, with his air of confident authority. As she saw him coming through the tables, acknowledging the salutations of acquaintances with genial waves of the hand, she suddenly felt immeasurably relieved.

But his opening remarks were in his stern-father manner. 'What the hell those young men are doing, letting you gad about at night, with all those thugs lying in wait for you, I can't for the life of me imagine.' He sat down and ordered brandy, with more for Jenny.

'They must be out of their minds. Where are they?'

'They've found out where the Russian has his base—and where they think Mrs Ingram is being held. It's a villa at Kalami, on the southern end of the bay, with its own quay.'

'I know it. Been there lots of times. It's owned by an actor feller now, and he's let it on a long lease to an Italian. Ye-e-es, that's a very likely springboard for the exercise. Little chance of observation at this time of year. But it'd be a hell of a risk to cross the straits at night without being seen by either a Greek or an Albanian patrol. Unless, of course, they've got radar ... That's it, radar. They'd stay in the bay, blanketed by the headland, until they knew the way was clear and then make their dash and hope the searchlights wouldn't show 'em up. It's only a couple of miles, after all, and there's a motor-yacht that's been let with the villa. Thirty-five footer, petrol-driven. The only snag would be the moon.'

'There's no moon now,' Jenny pointed out. 'And just listen to the rain.'

'That makes the whole operation much more likely, because rain would diffract the searchlights.' Barnard downed the rest of his brandy. 'I rather thought the car would come in handy,' he said. 'It's parked over there. Excuse me a moment.' He rose and walked briskly away to the manager's office, to return with a waiter carrying an outsize umbrella.

'Take my arm, my dear, and keep close.'

With the rain thundering down they crossed the road and found his Cortina. 'I hope you're right in thinking you've got rid of your trailers,' said Barnard, 'because if they saw us going to naval HQ they'd guess we're on to them, and warn the villa. The naval chaps will want to catch them red-handed.'

Jenny raised her voice above the noise of the heavy drops pattering on the umbrella. 'Is that where you're taking me? There's no need, Major, really. All I wanted was for you to ring the admiral and get me an interview with him. I can do the rest.'

'So you shall, m'dear. But it'll make it a lot quicker if I take you to him myself. I'm known around here, and they're aware I'm a sensible sort of bloke and don't start hares. I rang the admiral from the café. Told him I had reason to think there would be an illegal crossing getting underway from Kalami, so that he could take what action he thought fit. Now look here, young lady. I'm not going to get mixed up in this operation. Got to keep my nose clean if there's trouble afterwards. So I'll do what I've just said, but that's all. Leave you to do the rest. Afterwards—all I did was give you a lift on a rainy night, as far as other people are concerned. It's only old Steriotis who'll be in the know.'

'You're an angel, aren't you?' she said warmly, squeezing his arm.

'Nonsense,' said the major gruffly. 'Don't like the Russians, but more than that, I don't like young Greeks being conned into doing their dirty work for them. Hardly cricket, is it? Another thing I don't like,' he added, as they took the Corniche road and he switched the windscreen wipers to double speed, 'is fellers who'd kidnap a magnificent woman like Mrs Ingram in order to blackmail her husband. I wouldn't blame him, to tell you the truth, for anything he did to get her back. Sort of woman a man'd die for.'

Jenny gritted her teeth. 'Yes, Major,' she said humbly.

*      *      *

Admiral Steriotis was waiting for them in his office, a high-ceilinged room with a large window overlooking the sea. With him was an officer wearing a naval commando blouse with two and a half gold stripes on the shoulders. There were introductions, and coffee was brought in and served, but they were all anxious to get down to business. The admiral spoke in Greek, although his English was completely fluent. He wanted there to be no possibility of misunderstanding.

'When you called me, Major, I got through to my radar station, and they reported that the straits were clear at the moment, but that the heavy rain made conditions ideal for an illegal

220

crossing. Now, may I have your story in full? Lieutenant-Commander Metaxa will be in charge of the interception operation—if such action should be necessary.'

Barnard said, 'I'd like to stay, Admiral, but there are reasons why I don't want to get too closely involved at this stage. However, I have every confidence in this young lady, who is a diplomatic officer in our Athens Embassy. When it's all over, let's meet in the Club and I'll tell you more, for your ears only.' He winked, picked up his umbrella, shook hands with Metaxa and the admiral, and patted Jenny on the shoulder. Then he left the room, and Jenny began her story without delay, in Greek and as concisely as she could.

The admiral was not a man to be rushed. The war years, followed by the civil war, and the problems of deploying a small force against more powerful adversaries, had bred in him a blend of daring and caution. He interrupted Jenny several times, to get points clear.

She saw Metaxa glancing impatiently at his watch, and said, 'I'm sorry, Admiral, but I'm afraid it's a complicated story. If you agree, may I give you the operational outline first, and fill in the details later?'

He nodded. She went on, 'The main fact is that we suspect that a Soviet-hired motor-yacht based on the villa I mentioned at Kalami will be dropping Greek infiltration agents tonight off the Albanian coast, so that they can swim in without being spotted, using scuba equipment, land at deserted beaches, and make their way into the interior. There may or may not be an English lady aboard, the one who is being held as hostage by the KGB officer, Vlasov. We know that this man Vlasov has armed men under his command, and there may therefore be resistance to an interception.'

The two men looked at her, a little baffled. Neither had met a girl who talked like this before, and they were surprised at her calm assumption that her story would be accepted without question.

Then Metaxa said, 'When the yacht leaves Kalami, sir, we'll have to act very fast indeed, and it'll be better for my launch to be already at sea. If you agree, I'll take No 204 out and Miss Otfield can accompany me, for purposes of completing the brief and identifying the persons we may find on the yacht.'

The admiral thought for a little. Then he nodded.

They drove through the blinding rain at a speed which only a driver completely familiar with the twisting road would risk in such conditions, and reached the port of Kassiopi, at the north-eastern tip of the island.

Five minutes later, clad in a yellow storm-jacket and waterproof cap, and very glad of both, because the rain was still heavy, Jenny had crossed the quay from the naval car to the patrol launch. Metaxa hurried her down below and went on to the bridge. She could hear commands and pounding feet overhead and then a roar, as the engines sprang to life. A rating came to summon her to the bridge.

Metaxa was quite aware that he cut a dashing figure as he stood peering through the spray-screen with its rotary wiper at the darkness ahead. He said, 'Come closer, Miss Otfield, so that I can hear your story.'

All distances on Corfu are short, and it was only five miles by sea from Kassiopi to the Koloura headland. The rain was diminishing now, but clouds still covered the moon, hiding the coastlines on either side, so that it seemed as though the launch, her lights extinguished and her engines at SLOW, was gliding quietly in a black void over an endless stretch of oily water. The only point of reference in the pervading darkness was the radar screen, with its revolving arm revealing the coastlines in flickering succession, and here and there a blip of light as the beam passed over a vessel at anchor.

Metaxa was watching keenly, and he spotted a blip in mid-channel and was turning the helm before Jenny realized what had happened. After a minute he said sharply, 'That's odd; she seems to be stationary. Surely they're too far from the Albanian coast to put the divers overboard.' He gave an order to the young lieutenant at his side. 'Assemble the boarding party on deck.' The launch increased speed, and Metaxa snapped out another order.

The shape of the yacht flashed out of the darkness ahead, totally exposed in the glare of the searchlight. She was lying helpless, becalmed on the smooth water, only three hundred yards away.

Jenny seized Metaxa's arm. 'Are you going alongside?' she asked anxiously.

'If they give trouble, of course. Go below, please.' He pushed her towards the companionway, but Jenny twisted away from him.

'Last time we met Vlasov he used a grenade,' she said quickly.

'A grenade? You're not serious?' He was impatient now; there was work for him to do.

'I'm quite serious, Commander. Listen, *please*. It happened last night, and it killed one of his own men. But it was meant to sink our boat.'

Metaxa said slowly, 'Are you really sure? Do you know what a grenade looks like?'

'Of course I do—I've used them on a training exercise. And I've seen the damage they can do, especially to boats.'

'I'll have to take your word for it, but I'll look very foolish if you're wrong.' He called to the lieutenant. 'I'm going to close very slowly. Man the machine-gun. They may have grenades.'

The naval launch was brought to a halt thirty yards from the yacht. They could see a fair-haired man standing in the cockpit, but no-one else. Metaxa picked up a loud-hailer and shouted, 'Muster all hands on deck. At once, or we fire.' Three sailors, and six men in gleaming wet-suits, emerged from below and clambered onto the deck. The man with fair hair remained where he was. One of the sailors, an older man, spoke to him, but he shook his head and remained staring at the launch.

'You there,' shouted Metaxa. 'Get on deck.' The launch was drifting closer. Nikitch turned as if to obey. His right hand was hidden.

Suddenly, the grey-haired sailor shouted at him, 'Stop! They're *Greeks*,' and when the other ignored him and swung up his arm the sailor crossed himself and leapt down on him.

As if at a signal, the men in wet-suits plopped into the water like frogs off a lily-leaf. Jenny's heart sank. Once submerged, they could get away and make for the Albanian coast—although without survival packs they would not get far.

There was a thump in her ears, and the air around the stern of the yacht was full of flying scraps of clothing, and blood, and bits of flesh.

She turned her head, feeling sick, and Metaxa held her arm. 'Thanks,' he said simply. 'Now I've got to alert the shore-party.'

'Shore-party?' she stammered, still hearing

that awesome thump, and seeing what had happened to the two men struggling in the open cockpit.

'You don't think we were going to attack the villa from the sea without making sure there was no escape by land? There's a section of marines in the woods behind the house. What we've just seen is proof of what you suspected, so I'll tell them to close in and signal when they're ready to storm the house. But first I must deal with this yacht.'

While speaking he had been drawing closer, and the launch now lay alongside the yacht. The lieutenant sprang across the gap and gave one glance into the cockpit. He turned away hastily to give orders to the sailors on the fore-deck. 'Get the pump working,' he shouted—and then realized that if the engines had stalled there would be no power. 'Hand-pumps, I mean. You must have some. Get going.'

Metaxa called down to him, 'What's the damage, Nikki?'

'She's badly holed, Captain.' He looked down, and saw two pairs of black web-fingered hands clasping the gunwale. A moment later the two men had climbed over the side. They pulled off their helmets and looked up at him, sheepishly.

'Don't stand there idle!' he cried. 'Start baling. Use your headgear.'

Metaxa was down to the waist of the launch,

looking over the side at the damage caused by the explosion. 'I'll get you a tarpaulin,' he said to the lieutenant. 'The divers can rig a patch over the hole.'

Jenny was helping to tie rope lengths to the corners of a piece of canvas when she saw, with startled eyes, four rubber heads appear together over the gunwale. A marine covered the divers as they climbed into the launch. But they showed no aggressive intentions. On the contrary. One of them took off his helmet, caught sight of Jenny, and said politely, *'Kalispera, Kyría.'* Then they, too, had to cross to the cockpit of the yacht and start baling.

The yacht had been searched, and all those of Vlasov's men who were still alive were working docilely under guard to keep her afloat. On Metaxa's orders a tow-rope was rigged. Jenny felt a surge of relief. At least, the landing operation had been thwarted. That was one part of the job completed. But what was happening at the villa? She looked towards the shore. The little bay of Kalami was out of sight behind the Koloura headland, which she could see now in the starlight. There was still a bank of cloud over the moon, but the rain had stopped at last.

Ten minutes later they had slipped the tow and were steering towards Kalami, with lights out. The engines were at half-speed as they slid through the smooth water, aiming for the further side of the little bay, where they could

227

see the lights on the upper floors of the villa.

Suddenly, from the woods behind the building, a rocket streaked up into the sky and burst in a silver shower. Metaxa increased speed and leaning to one side pressed a switch and gripped the guiding handle of the searchlight fitted above his head. The beam lingered for a moment, seeking, and then found its target. The whole white facade of the villa was bathed in brilliant light.

The sound of a shot came across the water, followed without pause by a short burst of rapid fire. Then silence.

## CHAPTER SIXTEEN

Vlasov was in a bad way. Grant bent down to look at him, and tilted his head so that the blood would flow from his mouth and ease his choked breathing. He showed no signs of pain, but the red stain across the front of his shirt was spreading. He stared up at Grant's grim face and said softly, 'What happened to the yacht? . . . Was it you? . . . Sabotage?'

'Honey in the petrol,' said Grant. 'There was a lot of it in the storeroom.'

'Honey.' Vlasov's voice was faltering. 'Cunning . . . aren't you, Grant? But there's something you don't know, even yet . . . You . . .' He laughed, and choked, and this time

228

there was no way to help him.

Grant closed the staring pale eyes. Then he reached into the man's pocket and pulled out documents in Russian. He stood up.

Kellezi had been taken away. A man in naval uniform was watching Grant curiously. He said, 'Metaxa, Commander, Greek Navy. According to Mr Ingram this man was threatening to have you cut into little pieces, Mr Grant. You're very forgiving.'

'He was only doing his job. As you did yours, Commander, with great efficiency, and I'm most grateful. Where's Ingram?'

'Upstairs, with his wife. I left them together.'

'Was it he who found her room?'

'Yes. It's the second on the right as you come from the stairs.'

Grant stood for a time by the window, thinking. There was a lot to work out. Then he went into the hall and saw Jenny just coming down the stairs. She reached the bottom and stood uncertainly, looking forlorn. Then she caught sight of Grant and ran to throw her arms around him. 'Oh Luke, it's so good to see you again.'

He held her away from him and looked down into her unhappy face. 'It was seeing them together, I suppose,' he said, stroking her hair.

'Yes, it brought it all back. It sounds terrible but I could have wished Clare . . .'

'Of course. But listen, Jenny. The situation may not be quite what it seems. There's something I've got to prove, and I need your help.' Briefly, he explained, and she nodded, puzzled. 'Don't ask me why,' he added. 'You'll know soon enough.'

Together they went up to the floor above and along a broad passage with bedroom doors opening from it. One of them had been forced open and was still ajar. Grant went in and took a quick glance at the inside of the lock. There was no key, but he had hardly expected to find it there. Jenny joined him.

Ingram and Clare were standing by the window, hand in hand. Grant took a deep breath. Everything depended on how he played a very weak hand. 'Vlasov's dead,' he said curtly, and to Clare, not Ingram. 'But he talked to me first.' It was the almost imperceptible narrowing of her eyes that told him he was right.

Jenny had apparently been looking out of the window. 'My God!' she cried suddenly. 'Look at the yacht.'

As Clare and Ingram peered out into the night Grant picked up the small lizard handbag that was lying on the bed and turned its contents onto the counterpane.

'There's nothing out there, Jenny,' said Ingram, amused. 'You're getting jumpy, and it's not surprising.'

Behind him, he heard Grant's voice. 'But

230

this is.' He was holding up a key.

'What on earth are you doing with my bag, Luke?' asked Clare sharply. 'Give it to me, please . . . I want it now.'

'What is this key?' asked Grant harshly.

With scarcely a moment's hesitation she said, 'It's the one belonging to our villa, of course.'

'No it's not,' said Ingram smiling. 'It's a different type altogether. But what is this about, Luke? Some kind of joke?'

Grant crossed the room and slid the key into the lock. Then he turned it. 'It fits perfectly. Was it on the outside of the door when you came to this room, Roger?'

'Of course not. I had to break the door in.' He looked at Grant anxiously.

'I thought so. Clare wasn't Vlasov's prisoner here, Roger. She was never a prisoner at all. She just locked herself in when she heard you coming.' He turned to Jenny, who was running her fingers over the lining of the bag. 'Have you found something?'

'There's a gap in the stitching,' she said, 'and look.' She held out two small plastic envelopes, one white and the other blue. 'I've seen these before. The blue is one of the KGB inks, and the other's the developer. It's a top-security ink, Luke,' she added, without expression. 'They must have thought highly of her.'

Clare was watching the scene without

speaking. It was as if a shutter had come down, and behind it her quick mind was working, seeking a way out. Ingram's face was dead pale.

He said slowly, 'So that's how you communicated with him. Those letters to 'school-friends' I never met. There was one in Athens, I remember. And of course he was on the courier run to London for a time.'

She said appealingly, 'I was helpless, Roger. Nikolai had me completely in his power, but I couldn't tell you. The Office would never have allowed us to marry, and that's what I wanted so much.'

Ingram smiled bitterly. 'I might believe that story from anyone else, but not from you, Clare. You wouldn't be blackmailed easily. It explains a lot of things I didn't understand. You were his mistress before we met, I imagine.'

Her manner changed completely. 'And if I was? It's no crime in Britain to be a Soviet agent, unless you're caught passing classified information. And you'll never get me under the OSA, Roger dear, unless you admit telling me Office secrets. And what a lot you did tell me, at that!' With deliberate cruelty she added, 'Poor innocent! Of course he was my lover before we met, and that was the point. He set a trap for you, with me as bait—and how enthusiastically you fell into it! I did a lot for Nikolai. He was a man!' She started, and looked at Grant. 'I don't believe he told you anything about me before he died.'

'You're quite right. He didn't. He just said there was something I didn't know. And I guessed it must be about you.'

'You . . .' Her face had lost all serenity, all charm. 'You're clever, Lucas Grant, but you won't find you can charge me with anything.'

'Oh, I think so. But what's certain is that the Greeks will.'

'*The Greeks?*' She slumped down on the bed, her face pale. 'I'm a British subject. You can't hand me over to the Greeks.'

'Oh yes, we certainly can. You were an accessory to the murder of a Greek national, Katastari, and that's a capital charge for a start. I wonder if you know what that means, in Greece? And then there's your involvement in the agent-running operation. I think that could be proved.' She glanced at her husband, but his isolation from her was almost tangible. 'I couldn't stand it, Roger; I'd go mad.' He turned his face away. She appealed to Grant. 'Luke, I couldn't stand being locked up in a stinking cell.'

'That,' he said flatly, 'would be the least of your worries.'

'But if I tell you everything I know. If I agree to collaborate completely. As Jenny said, the KGB did think very highly of me. I'd be an important defector. Surely you can persuade the Greek authorities to let me go to England?

You've done them a good turn, haven't you?'

'I could try,' said Grant slowly, 'but only if you talk first. Now. Everything you know, from the beginning—about Vlasov, and his plans, his contacts, the communications—everything. If you try to play down your own role I shall know.' He went to the writing table and spread out some sheets of paper taken from the drawer. 'There was a pen among the things in your handbag. Start now.'

Ingram stood rigid, looking down at his wife. The light caught the gleam of her hair. He said slowly, 'Do what he says. I don't want to know anything about it. Not now.' He left the room.

Jenny stood irresolute. Then she said, 'I think I'd better go to him, don't you?' Grant nodded.

\*       \*       \*

It was the following afternoon. Grant was packing his bag when Jenny knocked at his door. 'Come in.'

She sat down and watched him for a moment. Then, 'They're sending out an Under-Secretary to negotiate with the Foreign Ministry in Athens. There's a D-notice on the news, for the time being. The vice-consul's been marvellous, and he's enjoying himself. That's all on my net. What do you know, Luke?'

234

'Clare's in the Old Fort, and that's where I finished the interrogation. I got quite a lot from her, but there may be much more—I just couldn't hold off the Greek security people longer. But they've been very good about the whole thing, and seem grateful to us for saving them from a very embarrassing situation vis-a-vis the Albanians. They may waive the murder charge. It'd be a tricky one to make stick. So we may be left to deal with Clare in London—and that'd be a dicey one, too. We've precious little evidence that'd stand up in the Old Bailey, and both the Office and our people will lean over backwards to play the whole thing down.'

'Luke, how did you guess about Clare?'

'I started with those last words of Vlasov's, and worked it out. The logical male mind,' he added teasingly. 'Everything gradually fitted in. Who was it, besides Roger, who could have known just where and when he and Spiro were to meet? Clare. Kellezi's story about finding out that Spiro had telephoned to a Paleocastritsa number, on the strength of which Vlasov took his yacht right round the island to Paleocastritsa Bay, sounded too far-fetched. But I learned last night that Clare had a radio set at the villa, well hidden, for communication with Andreas and Vlasov, and she had plenty of prior warning of what Ingram was going to do. There was another puzzle. We worked out that Vlasov, as soon as he'd got away from his wrecked boat, must have rung his stooge at the villa and told him to get Clare away fast. Time was essential, because we might have turned up at any moment. But Clare had taken time to change into day clothes and pack a suitcase. Why? Because there *wasn't* a stooge in the villa. There was no need for one. It was typical of Clare's calculating brain to reason that there was time for a quick pack. She did just that, apparently, and waited in a side-turning until we'd driven past, before continuing on her way to Kalami. It was always Clare who was the answer to the puzzling bits. Remember, Roger was so baffled by the leaks that he even thought you were guilty.'

'Yes. He told me what Spiro had told him, and apologized abjectly for suspecting me. Poor Roger! He's going to resign, of course, but he'll still have to face an investigation first. Your Internal Security sharks will have a ball. My affair with him will be scrutinized, to see if any blame attaches to me. That'll be hard to take, Luke.'

He saw the revulsion in her face, but there was determination, too. She went on, 'I've got to help him. He needs me. He says that without me to help him now he can't face the future.'

'So that's settled, is it?' said Grant bitterly. 'Back to square one with Roger? There'll be only one difference. At least you know now

236

that he is the marrying kind.' He regretted the words as soon as he had said them.

'Don't be silly. I'll help him get through this wretched phase, if the Firm will let me, but afterwards, I don't ever, ever, want to see him again.'

'So you say, Jenny.'

'So I mean. And I shan't change my mind. As far as Roger is concerned, you might say my eyes are opened.' She looked up at him fleetingly, and changed the subject. 'When Vlasov captured you and Roger, and was going to drop you both off the Albanian coast, why did Clare bother to go on playing her part? That's what I can't understand.'

'Because she was still a KGB asset and there was the possibility that you would both survive. She'd have gone back to England and winkled her way back into SIS circles.'

'So that was it. She was a smooth operator, Luke, I'll give her that. You took a chance when you raided her bag.'

'Actually, by then I was quite sure. There was another clue I didn't tell you about. Stand up, Jenny. Now turn round. Right. Now, I've come up behind you suddenly and put my arm round your waist, like this.'

'I rather like it.'

'That fits, because I'm Vlasov and you're Clare.'

'That isn't what I meant.'

'Be quiet, and listen. I'm using you as a

shield, while I threaten those intrusive foreigners Grant and Ingram with a gun. But they're armed too. So if you're on their side, what do you do?'

'Bend down, of course, and leave you a sitting target. There's nothing to stop me, with just your arm round my waist . . . Which I like.'

'And that's just it,' explained Grant. 'Vlasov *knew* Clare wouldn't do that, or he'd have got his hand round her throat.'

'You can do that, too, if you want.'

'He knew she'd stand straight and act as his screen. But any normal person, even without SIS training, would have ducked, as you said, if only out of fear. There. Are you satisfied?'

'Not by a long way.' She turned slowly, and put her arms round his neck. 'Are you?'

He bent and kissed her, and found he had no wish to stop. It really did not surprise him. It went on for some time.

Then Jenny stirred, and said in his ear. 'Have you got to catch that plane?'

'Yes. But I'm not going to. Shall we go to Averof's for dinner?' He kissed her. 'Towards evening, when we're quite ready?'

'Yes, please.'

'And then we'll have coffee and ouzo on the Liston, and come back here. And be together again. And let tomorrow take care of itself.'

'Yes, please.'

We hope you have enjoyed this Large Print book. Other Chivers Press or G.K. Hall & Co. Large Print books are available at your library or directly from the publishers.

For more information about current and forthcoming titles, please call or write, without obligation, to:

Chivers Press Limited
Windsor Bridge Road
Bath BA2 3AX
England
Tel. (01225) 335336

OR

G.K. Hall & Co.
P.O. Box 159
Thorndike, Maine 04986
USA
Tel. (800) 223-2336

All our Large Print titles are designed for easy reading, and all our books are made to last.